BRONTE WILDE

BRONTE WILDE

FANNY HOWE

grand IOTA

Published by
grand**IOTA**

2 Shoreline, St Margaret's Rd, St Leonards TN37 6FB
&
37 Downsway, North Woodingdean, Brighton BN2 6BD

www.grandiota.co.uk

First published in the USA by Avon Books, 1976
First UK (revised) edition, 2020
Copyright © Fanny Howe, 1976, 2020. All rights reserved.

Typesetting & book design by Reality Street

A catalogue record for this book is available from the British Library

ISBN: 978-1-874400-75-2

Bronte Wilde

When I was two years old a nun named John brought me across the Atlantic Ocean to Boston. It was a time when children were casually transferred from one person to the next. So I arrived in America as a ward of Catholic charity, and was soon after adopted by the Casements. They were affluent, middle-aged, childless; and affectionate without making physical contact. Both were practicing psychiatrists. Alice worked with disturbed adolescents and Henry worked with disturbed adults. Her office was on the ground floor of our townhouse, as you know; and his office was in a building around the corner on Commonwealth Avenue. Remember there was a big ugly plant and a green and gloomy waiting room for the children to the left of our front door where the dining room should have been.

When I was four years old and curious about pregnant women and the origins of life, Alice told me that I was nurtured in another woman's body, not her own, and that she had picked me out of a row of babies-for-sale because I had a wise little face. It was a time when people tended to pretend rather than confess, and being adopted, like being divorced, carried a stigma. So it was brave of her to tell me these facts. The effect on me was to her advantage. I felt I must be good and obedient all the time, in case she should change her mind about my wisdom and return me to the agency. I was grateful. They had done me an enormous favor by feeding, clothing and housing me. I am not saying this with any bitterness, because my feelings sprang from an insight that might be shared by any biological child. Yet I also sensed that I lived in a world in which I did not belong, would never belong.

They named me Mary. I called them Alice and Henry instead of Mummy and Daddy, and, as friends, we got along very well. I always wanted someone to call Mother but I also sensed that indifference had shadowed the narrow lips of the bearer of that name while her arm drooped protectively but casually before my infant body. I know at that time I was ashamed of how old my guardians were compared with the other parents, and it made it all the easier for me to disclaim any blood relationship with them. But they told me all that they could about those first two years of my life.

I met you finally at home. It was a rainy day, pouring and gray. I was sitting in my room watching my goldfish in a bowl in the window. My brain seized with a delirium that was already familiar to me. The rain as a backdrop dribbling on the glass behind the swift red fish – green weeds and hairy algae – in some way saved me the way music did. My parents would say I was 'in an alternative universe'.

Then there was the gentle knock, Alice's respectful touch. I called to her to come in. You were with her.

Mary, I want you to meet Honey Figgis. She'll be starting at Mystic with you next week.

We said awkward *Hi*'s and Alice left us alone. You were dressed sloppily, I am sure. Falling socks, wet loafers, a sweater full of holes. Still, I know my first impression was one of glaring beauty.

I'm one of her patients, you announced.

Oh, she has lots of them our age, I told you.

My problem is I'm scared of school. I don't know why.

Mystic is okay, I said, and you'll be in my class.

You looked around the room suspiciously, then gave me a winningly secretive grin.

Where's the bathroom? you asked.

I took you down the hall and went in with you while you peed. I looked at my face in the mirror and wished it was yours.

Is Dr Casement your grandmother?

No, my guardian. I'm adopted.

Oh you lucky!

Your heavy-lidded, deep-set, long-lashed eyes flashed while I quickly told you my story; it was a kind of nervous tic that was to be your mark. I don't know how you did it, the action was too quick, but when I tried to imitate it, I looked psychotic. Long legs, straight blonde hair, a bony face and thin sculpted lips. That was you. Remember how well we got to know each other? Every hair, mole, dent and shadow recorded in cars, subways, dressing rooms, bedrooms, bathrooms, parks, school hallways. We knew each other better than we knew ourselves.

B oston. Beantown. A grim name for a grim city. Brick. A fishy smell on certain easterly breezes. Gray lumps of puddingstone. Ash, elm, chestnut, sycamore, maple, pine. Splashes of water. Somber rooms with low lights, books, a sense of enclosure; even the streets are like indoor spaces. We lived on the block of Gloucester Street that lies between Marlboro and Commonwealth. Institutions abound. Everywhere is a sign: schools for secretaries, nurses, for social workers, offices for psychiatrists and dentists, and some apartments still domestic and fashionable.

Twice a week, down the street on the corner of Beacon, I took piano lessons. First with Stewart Loomis, long, tweedy, egg yolk on his tie, a half-zipped fly. Then with Melvin Marchand who drooled, and finally with Ramon who taught me until the scandal. From an early age I understood that music would be my main occupation and would serve to gratify Alice and Henry and pay them back for their generosity. Fortunately I was a music lover myself. Like those goldfish in the bowl, the notes on the page circled around in a corner of myself, wholly self-contained.

Alice and Henry took me to the Symphony every Friday afternoon. They yearly gave money to the Conservatory but I was their real contribution to the arts. Most of my afternoons were passed in the rich red 'music room' adjoining my bedroom. I practiced while snow, or rain, or patterns of sunlight drifted beyond my geranium plants. The worn Turkish carpet, smell of books, and a soft yellow lamp provided an atmosphere of resonant calm which will of course never return. On Sundays we went to lunch with Henry's mother and afterwards I was alone again with a book or the piano. It was a post-Victorian childhood trying to survive the twentieth century.

Henry had a slight stammer and a stoop that gave his

tall, lean figure an air of attention, sympathy, gentility. Pigeon-gray crew cut hair, a long compressed face, spectacles halfway down his nose. He twiddled his thumbs while listening: He had the air of a professor far more than a psychiatrist; he even rode a bicycle. He called me Maryberry.

Alice, in my mind, is autumnal, orange, marigold, sharp, spicy, tailored in plaid tweeds and soft cashmeres, a row of mother-of-pearl always worn at her throat, a scent of tobacco, sensible shoes, buck teeth, eyes set in heavy loose lids and fatigue circles, her cheeks heavy, her voice crumpled like a man's voice from smoking. She spent most of her spare time in bed, wrapped in a pale quilted dressing gown, the curtains drawn, smoking and reading. I stood a few feet away from her bed when speaking to her.

They never quarreled. They seemed to have nothing to quarrel about, yet I can't exactly say, in retrospect, that theirs was that miraculous situation called a happy marriage. It was functional, compatible and passionless. They were like siblings. Alice was committed to her work; they went out or entertained at least three nights a week; a woman cleaned and often cooked for them. But I cannot say that she was 'fulfilled'. Often she seemed sad. (Or maybe sadness is happiness since it is so interesting.) They were reticent about themselves, so reticent, in fact, that I knew little about their youth or their past. I would sit at the kitchen table with them and kick the legs of my chair until they began to talk to cover up the irritating sound. They never told me to stop. I kicked in a code only I could crack, but when I heard the trailing whine of a trolley coming down the tracks outside, only then would my kicks subside, and the music of the metal wheels took over, leading to something resembling a memory.

Why do they call you Honey? I asked.

Honora is my disgusting real name.

Do you have sisters or brothers?

No, my parents hate each other.

What does your father do?

He's a professor.

Of what?

History. I have a dog too.

I just have fish, I confessed.

You spent the night at my house first and began in the dark to narrate your autobiography. I remember your raw whispers beside my ear, my legs hanging out the side of the bed for fear of physical contact with you. You said your father had crash-landed during the War in Sicily and was rescued by a family of Fascist Catholics. One of them was a beautiful woman whom he got pregnant. She was forced by her family to give the baby away, but he took the baby himself and brought her back to America with him at the end of the war.

That's why my mother hates me, you concluded, not

noticing the violence of my reaction to this narrative, this utter fraud. I actually concealed my rage from you by running to the bathroom and grinding my teeth and tearing at my hair in the darkness there. You had twisted my own true story into your fantasy!

When I returned to the bed, you added to your conclusion this important detail: 'That's also why my father has those pictures of Mussolini and Hitler in his study.'

Do you remember those endless whisperings night after night? To this day I find the sound of a whisper repellant, almost evil.

But then I whispered aloud a huge fake future for you, and one for me, and in this way shifted your focus onto that and away from the fraudulent past. We lay in my bed sometimes until the sun rose pink and gold in the room like two short-term inmates exchanging fantasies about the future.

I saw your mother a while back. Browsing through books in Providence, she wore bedroom slippers and a trench-coat. It was snowing outside and her ankles were red. In fact it was her slippers and ankles that I recognized first under a stall of books, and then her face, its high flush, her hair dyed blonde. I rushed away from there before she could see me.

My mother doesn't care if I smoke, you say, taking a deep drag. Have a weed.

I say no, and it makes you mad.

You flounce away, leaving me in front of Hayes-Bickford. So I take the subway home to my piano and see my face on the black underground window, swaying, frizzy black hair, and a pale center. I am overweight and disgusted with myself. Often you make me feel this way: too heavy to soar, a bear keeping up with a deer.

But you need my slow dark presence at your side, especially at first at school. You stick by me and by the door, claustrophobic in the classroom, crushed by the role of silent listener. To be lectured to: it makes you tremble and sweat. You have no defense against the voice of authority. The palms of your hands slide across the roof of your desk. You ask to be excused from a class at least three times a day, when you hide in the bathroom smoking. The teachers know you have a problem, and you are so rich and pretty, you are treated by one and all with care.

One afternoon Alice came to me and said she wanted to have a little talk. It was a winter day, dreary, void of snow or cheer, and I was hiding in my music room with my homework, probably waiting for you to call. Alice was always intent on avoiding her professional role in her relationship with me. She never, if possible, had 'heart-to-heart' talks. Now she asked me how I was doing in school.

Fine, I said, why?

No reason. I'm glad you're doing well.

She smiled and then began to cast out questions, like the lines of fishermen in mountain lakes, a hissing flight, a splash, and silence. She stood, knee-deep in her own motives, waiting.

How is Honey these days? she asked first.

Fine.

Do you see much of her at school?

Yes, a lot.

And afterwards what do you do together?

Just hack around her house, or the Square. Sometimes Libby and Henny come too.

That's good ... How's the piano coming?

Okay.

Do you like Marchand?

No.

I didn't think so. Well, I'm starting you with a new man over at the Conservatory. He will come here to teach you. He's supposed to be excellent. Ramon Diaz — he must be Spanish.

I was happy to leave Marchand, but she had conveyed more than this switch to me, and I was vaguely distressed by the way she did so. While she wanted me to feel her endless understanding as a liberating force, she also wanted to manipulate my life. Perhaps she felt I was spending too much time with you. She would never come out and say so. I quite rightly was kept in the dark about your relationship with her, but it made me uneasy to be so ignorant.

The girls in school were a loud and undisciplined crowd. Arrogance, crude humor, and a spirit of individualism prevailed during our hours there. We had nothing but contempt for our teachers. Even those we admired, we admired with a kind of condescension reserved for those who could not live without us. The mothers, by and large, did not work, except voluntarily for charity or for occupation, visiting sick beds or reading to desperate children or donating cash to depoliticized peace and poverty. Teachers were hired along with cooks and housekeepers, to do the dirty work.

I was never entirely convinced by this attitude since I always felt I had been bought, not born, and I identified condescension with good fortune at a very early age. The gospels of Mark and Marx seem to have been born in me as a genetic trait. At the same time I did not want to seem dreary, a killjoy in the middle of fun. If I protested a cruelty, I saw my friends recoil; so the desire to be loved usually won out. I am ashamed at how often I went along with the crowd in tormenting a teacher or babysitter or working person. But I have also paid.

The Mystic School is small, brick, rustic, built before the turn of the century as a finishing school. We suffered through years of English history. The Wars of the Roses were far more intensely studied than the American Revolution. Five years of Latin and seven of French were requisites. The only attention given to a country outside Europe was to mention its produce and its use (oil, chocolate, coffee beans, rice, etc.). We had a small field for hockey and a small gym for basketball. There were no more than twelve girls in a class. Boys had no part in our activities until we hit thirteen when organized social dances were held in respective private school gymnasiums, chaperoned by mothers.

We were expected to go on to one of the best colleges for women. We were expected to sustain a point of view toward the world that would assure our own security in it. What we would learn we could not forget – not the facts, but the interpretation of the facts. Like everyone else, we forgot names and dates quickly having nowhere practical to apply this information, but we had a method for dealing with the world, unconsciously acquired, difficult to abandon.

And while I have turned against it altogether since, I can see that the parochial atmosphere has some advantage in that it supplies a feeling of tribal purpose to those endless hours of education, otherwise absent. However, when some girl did not fit in to the complete effort, she was savaged.

You were judged as crazy, spoiled, undisciplined, a liar, a bad influence on me, a child of an alcoholic and a lecher. People were jealous of your beauty and frightened of your wholeheartedness. I protected you just by standing in your shadow. To every neurotic, or erotic, act on your part, I offered a soft-spoken excuse; for the meaning of love is just that – making excuses for the beloved.

Meanwhile I was perceived as being as common as a glass of cold milk.

Then Ramon entered our lives. He came to my house in a literal blizzard; his black coat and black hair sparkled. I had expected an old man and while he, in his twenties, was certainly a grown-up and inaccessible, he epitomized romance. Straight black hair, a sallow complexion, full cynical lips and melancholy eyes (not to mention his accent). I wanted to be Wanda Landowska or die. Of course, Alice never missed a trick, took my excitement in with a glance, and saw it would work to her advantage. No more complaints about practicing at night! (Boston, when your shadows slip over my back, I feel you saying: I thought we got rid of her, I thought she'd never come back. What a pathetic joke. And, in return, I can tell you I had hoped you'd been removed from all maps. How can you still exist, your stiff conventions, your prisons of brick and cobblestone, statue, gold dome, and hill, your containment of my childhood? You scare me!)

That winter I hibernated with my piano and sheets of music. I played 'The Flight of the Bumblebee' for our friends at school on the piano in the gym, impressing everyone. It was hard for you and for others to understand how I had ever endured practicing. Nonetheless you envied the skill.

And now I had Ramon insisting on daily reiterations of the most basic and boring duty: scales. I was not allowed to improvise or to attempt any music he had not selected. He was humorless and tyrannical – just your type as I see it now. For his approval I was obedient, I improved.

April, your fifteenth birthday. May, you met him. You came specifically for that purpose and waited out my lesson in my bedroom. I left you writing a sonnet at my desk, your hair falling on your hand. (You were writing those days in sonnet form, about Apollo and Clytie, Diana, blossoms, snow and desire.) I slipped into the other room to meet Ramon at the piano. You must have listened to me play, showing off for him and for you in the safety of my own home.

Smell the haunted magnolia, wafting through the open

kitchen window. The little tree, hunched, like you, an explosion of pinks, bees humming, where we met for tea and cinnamon toast after the lesson was over. We murmured, we blew into our cups, no mad chatter, but a pleasing conspiracy of mutual smiles and flattery. Ramon, Napoleonic, lounged in his chair, begged us to meet him in Harvard Square for pastries after school. He balanced his attentions, made sure each one of us had our fill of his glances. For this spell, he dropped the virtuoso manner, strict teacher that he was, and talked to me as a young woman, a pal.

So we met him at the Patisserie, where we could sit outside and drag on the soft spring air. Apricot tarts and tea. He told us his history. Enchanted by tragedy: during the War he had hidden in the mountains of Spain with his father, a Leftist violinist. The family was reunited in Geneva, and there he grew up.

It's to Geneva I will return, he concluded, when my visa runs out.

When will that be? you cried.

He frowned and squeezed his lemon. Juice shot in my eye, and he applied the corner of a napkin to the spot in the tenderest way.

I have a year left, he said.

Why won't they let you stay forever? you asked.

They? Who? It's the law. I would have to marry a rich American woman to do that, he said and laughed pleasantly.

Then do. Marry one and stay.

No, Honey, he replied, I'm a simple man.

Rocking home on the subway, swinging from the straps, we dissected every word he said. He was The World, Suffering, Exile, Europe invading America. He was, also, of course, sexuality. His idle remark about marrying a rich woman was shrouded in insinuation. We conjured her up in fur and perfume, a wrestling match between good luck and bad. The sight of dogs mating in the Public Garden made us scream. But Ramon made you wiggle and sigh.

I was involved in these fantasies, but on the whole they were yours. You had devoured his entire being and claimed him for yourself. I wondered if he thought anything of you.

It was on a rainy spring day that I saw him openly discover you, at last. You came into the music room after my lesson was over as he put on his coat to go. You flew in with a poem you had written, and I saw him glance at you once, then twice, struck by your radiance. I felt as if I had been standing at a window watching a bird hop around looking for a crumb. When it finally found one, my expectations were gratified, as they were gratified and confused then by seeing Ramon discover you. Although I had never expected, or wanted, him to notice me like that, something burned in me, was humiliated by the moment. Immediately I decided he wasn't quite as great as I had thought he was. The look made him vulnerable – that is, equal to me in my own humiliation. You blushed and spread pink flowers around the room. You hid your face in the yellow jackets of your hair.

What's that in your hand? he asked.

Oh just a poem I wrote.

Someday you must let me see your poems, he said. Then he looked at his watch.

They're awful, you whispered.

I'm sure they're not, and I want to see them when I don't have to rush on to another lesson, Ramon said pleasantly. Okay?

Okay, you agreed.

When he was gone, I'm in love, I love him, was all you could say.

He's too old for you, I protested.

No he's not, he's just right.

Well, we'll see, I said, uneasily.

Before the school year was over, you had presented him with a little handmade book of your poems. All ten of them. A true labor of love, involving hours of meticulous care. He was effusive in his praise and gratitude, but clearly unnerved by the passion exploding from the object. My last two classes with him before the summer were held at the Conservatory, at his request, so you didn't see him for a long time again.

I really believed you would forget him during that summer. You went with your family to the Cape, sailed and swam and hung around the yacht club with a bunch of rich blonde friends. You went to dances and beach parties. (Remember when I came to visit you? You were ashamed of me: I was shoved into back seats of cars, told to sit on the dock and wait while you went sailing, I was left at home while you went to drive-in movies, and it was only an intervention of fate – I got appendicitis and went to recuperate with Lotte Lett, Alice's friend – which released us both from this grotesque occasion.) My only useful function during that time was to help you remember Ramon. You carved his head out of a piece of driftwood. You drew his profile ad infinitum. I was asked to remember the bend of his nose or the curl of his lips. On my return to Boston, with the new scar fresh on my abdomen, I was besieged with poems in the mail. All revolved around a lonely, dark Orphic figure, doomed to wander the world with the moon.

I was embarrassed by all of this. At some level I perceived that you were confusing a person with God. When Ramon returned, I blushed. But he was cool and strict and began to prepare me for a recital, and I had to pretend that the real Ramon had no relationship to the romantic Ramon, subject of all your school poems.

Autumn was brilliant that year with day after day of ice clear skies, sharp shadows. The leaves in the Gardens flamed. During classes you stared out the window, scribbling poems about mortality and love, dressed in black turtlenecks and black tights, your ears pierced, bohemian, dedicating all your poems to R.D. When most of the leaves had fallen he asked me where you were, and I told you this at lunch at school.

Do you dare me to take piano lessons from him? you asked, scarlet-cheeked.

Sure, go ahead, I said with my throat tightening.

Will he come to my house?

No, all his lessons are at the Conservatory now, I told you, so you'll have to go there.

I felt afterwards a deep grief, which I now can identify as renunciation. I could foresee your becoming an accomplished pianist, better than me, and once again – though I can never really know why – I found it necessary to urge you on towards the one thing that would make me suffer. It was as if I wanted to control the levers on my own destruction.

You arranged your class with Ramon to follow mine, so you would wait for me, and I would wait for you. I listened acutely to the faults in your scales decrease. You practiced obsessively. Ramon indicated nothing in the way of a love interest in you, but maintained a professional and polite attitude towards us both. It didn't matter. Your ability to focus on what you wanted was relentless.

It must have been February when the serious changes began. If it wasn't February in fact, it was February in spirit. The weather was gray, the streets slushy, the air nearly solid from cold. We went to your house on a gray Saturday afternoon. You had a secret to tell me. How to describe the squalor, gloom and intimacy of your house, I hardly know. Peeling wallpaper, big pots of dying plants, an aquarium full of foggy water and belly-up fish. Old furniture broken or maimed. Endless rooms, too much stuff. Your father had a study and bedroom in the attic. Once I went into his study and saw the pictures of Hitler and Mussolini you had mentioned. I thought you had been lying. It turned out (I asked Henry) your father was indeed a defender of Fascism after a war experience in the Sicilian mountains. Was the rest of that strange story true?

He and your mother didn't sleep or eat together. They didn't talk or plan together. Your father kept a mistress openly in the Hotel Continental in Cambridge, a place we often visited for some trace of her in the golden lobby. Jane Tabor, a middle-aged woman with a career. Your fat, blonde mother was sympathetic in the way of the down and out, attuned to people's troubles or else a vicious bitch, clever without tact or conscience. She cursed like a sailor and never got off the phone. The only person within range whom she never addressed was your handsome profile-conscious father. He rested his chin on his fingertips and stared musingly into space. He conveyed a feeling of melancholy insouciance ('It's all too much for me'), vanity, and cold-heartedness. Later I heard that he had begun as a brilliant philosophy student, who was deranged by his war experience. Yet he went on teaching courses, now in economics despite his extreme right pro-Fascist position and his supposed instability. I once heard him murmur, 'He who loves everyone loves no one,' a remark that came to describe him in my mind. The peculiar mix of privilege, education, booze, adultery and squalor confused me.

Still, until that one horrible day, I liked going home with you. Anarchy ruled the house. Between your mother's alcoholism and your father's indifference, we could do anything! Your bedroom had a slanted ceiling and a luminous view over the trees to Boston. We could see planes rising and landing in the blue, a spot of shining river. Your cocker spaniel, Sully (Prudhomme), servile, brown, lurked around your ankles.

I can see you now as you were on that Saturday afternoon: fingernails gnawed to the bone, a wizened anorexic look. You posed in the mirror trying to look first like Greta Garbo, then James Dean and finally Audrey Hepburn. Your father at one point stood at the door, on his way up to his retreat, and when he held out his arms to the image on the mirror, we both turned.

He entered, smiling coldly, placed one arm around each

of us. Enfolding us tight against his chest, he caressed my left breast and your right breast with the hard palms of his hands, caressed them as if our breasts were his, and he was alone in front of the mirror. It was as if he was seeing what it would feel like to be a woman checking herself for tumors! Then he pinched each of our nipples and turned and left at a clip.

You laughed: Isn't he a riot?

Your cheeks were flushed. I blushed thorns. In a flash you pushed me down on your bed and lay over me, twinned breast for breast, navel for navel, loin for loin. Laughing, between spastic intakes of breath, you grabbed around behind me, tickling me, and jerking against my resistance, my knees that buckled into your belly.

(She was excited by her father, she was turned on, with her sight turned off, eyes squeezed shut, laughing, and wrestling with my ribs. She held my hands down hard, pressed them into the covers of her bed, and didn't pretend to be tickling me then. Instead she gave a cry of anguish, calling *Daddy, Dad* and coming down hard and bony on my pelvis in her blue jeans.

Then she was up in a flash and the telephone rang at the same moment, she screamed at her mother to stay off the phone. Then she ran back into her bedroom and flung herself down on the bed and threw back an open triangle to climb into. There she hid, under the covers, her face. I sat on the floor with my knees up to my chest and my head down, praying Let that be all, let that be all, let that be all while the dog licked at the salt on my shoes. Nauseous, my skin crawled through the sequence of touches sustained in those speedy moments. I was a closed circuit, a thing with excess and no exits. Only two bad things had happened, and I knew there'd be a third.)

From under the covers you said, 'Ramon is taking me to the movies tomorrow afternoon. Can you believe it? He said he would call me at four. Today!'

Then you lifted your face out from under the bedclothes and your eyes flared for my response. 'Well?'

Your rose-flushed cheeks and wild hair only increased my sense of awkwardness and self-loathing, and I closed my face down on my knees again, saying nothing. 'You don't even care how it happened?' you cried. 'God, you're a killjoy! Well, I'll tell you. He was looking in my wallet and he saw my picture of James Dean and he asked if I had seen the movie and I said no, of course I couldn't say yes, and so he said he hadn't either and would I like to go with him.'

Well, let's hope he calls, I murmured.

Let's hope is right. If he doesn't, I'll go crazy.

And I should go home soon.

You can't. You're supposed to stay.

So we sat around waiting for him to call. It was horrible. The dog was terrified. You screamed at your mother to get off the phone and she threw a bedroom slipper at your head. When she hung up, it was four-fifteen and growing dark outside, and you took the phone in your room and howled into the household that no one should touch it but you. At five he still hadn't called and you kicked the dog in the stomach. He hid under the bed. I wanted to call Alice, to go home, but you wouldn't let me. Pale slashes of snow on the rooftops, an invisible moon. I heard your father creaking and rattling up the stairs, a martini in his hand, and imagined him coming from some sexy rendezvous. But you were chattering away insanely every detail of every hour you had passed with Ramon, asking me, again and again, to reassure you of his intentions.

He said he would call at four. I'm sure he did. I said that, didn't I? Maybe I made a mistake? Maybe he changed his mind?

I was getting scared. When things didn't work out for you, I wished they were going wrong for me instead. You couldn't handle disappointment the way I could, not at school or outside. Your eyes burned, your cheeks grew flushed as each hour passed. At around six, I was hungry but unable to leave. The dog rubbed you wrong, rubbed your legs. You pulled his skin and shoved him off, pulled him back and kneaded his wads of fur, tangles around his ears.

I'll kill myself, you said.

He'll call, don't worry.

No he won't. He obviously has someone else, that rich woman.

As scared as I was, I had no idea of how far you could go with your feelings and I watched your agitation increase with no sense of where it might lead you. I had never been a witness to your legendary bouts of violence. I was aware that your mother had abdicated all responsibility for her daughter, had handed you on to doctors and teachers long ago, so it didn't occur to me to seek her out through the stuffing and gloom of that house. (I still felt the effects of her violation on me, my clothes, my skin.)

The lights were on now, the sky a dark slate. You snatched up a pair of scissors on your bureau and grabbed the dog tight. And I watched you, the shears snapping, heard the dog scream and shriek, but never bite, as you cut off his whole ear. I remember double vision, sweat and rage overcoming me as I grabbed your hand and twisted the scissors away. The dog was screaming under the bed, his brown and bloody ear lying on the orange rug there. I remember you sitting quietly with the phone in your lap. It rang; it was Ramon. I ran into the hall and up the stairs to your father's attic. He was locked in the bathroom with the newspaper, and I had to shout through to tell him what had happened. He flushed the toilet promptly. But by the time we had come down to your room, you were smiling as if nothing had happened, having finished your talk with Ramon.

Your father sent me home and had the dog put to sleep that same night.

Your parents sent you back to Alice now every afternoon, in lieu of putting you in a hospital. I doubt if Ramon ever knew what happened that day and often wonder what he would have done if he had found out. You just told me how he took you to the movies on Sunday afternoon, then out for hot chocolate at Brighams afterwards, never laying a hand on you.

'But there was a strange feeling in the air, a sad feeling, I can't explain it, it had nothing to do with the horrible thing I did at home, all I know is I would die for him, I really would.'

Given his age and experience, I couldn't understand how he could lead you on like that. Your vulnerability should have been apparent to him. You were, you admitted, haunted by the dog, and couldn't sleep for thinking about him, and your eyes were darkly circled each day at school. I watched after you nervously as you gave away one possession after another. A scarf and a sweater to

Henny, a ring and three books to Libby, a bust of Keats to me, and more. Appeasement.

It is strange now to think how little was communicated between Alice and me and you on the subject of that night and your mental health. She must have been respecting some medical convention. But you too were silent about it and instead talked incessantly about your family and its neuroses and hypocrisies and secrets. Aunts, uncles, cousins were suddenly hauled up out of the darkness and inspected without pity.

Did you tell her about Ramon or not? I might ask after a session.

No. My Aunt Margaret was a complete alcoholic. Did I ever tell you about her? She was worse than my mother even. She crawled down Commonwealth Avenue in her slip one night, on her hands and knees. She told the police she had taken a Mickey Finn, whatever that is.

(This obsession with family traits was shared by many Wasps, I would learn in time. What they despised about their family was the only subject that truly interested them.)

I always waited upstairs for you, and often you slipped home afterward without saying goodbye. Finally in March you were passed along to a new psychiatrist somewhere else, and we were both freed from the need to discuss your treatment.

After one of my daily piano lessons, Ramon stood outside the conservatory and began to talk about his future. He wore his black overcoat and a blood red scarf. His lips were red, his cheeks pale. He puffed on a cigarette.

It looks like I'll be leaving in June, he said.

Oh no.

Yes, I'm off to Geneva.

That will be great.

I don't know, I suppose so.

He began to talk about his desire to tour the country before he left, to learn to build harpsichords, things like this. He addressed me as a fellow musician, it seemed, and this made me feel adult, briefly restoring my trust in him. He could always turn on the charm, inquiring about my progress with a certain piece in a way that made my work seem imperative to the development of all music through the ages.

Recitals make me so nervous, I confessed, I don't know if I want to perform at all.

They used to do that to me, too, he said, but I grew to realize that I was, like the piano, only a medium – for the angels, for the transference of sound – and my ego dissolved as soon as I was immersed in it. It must be like this with you. Think of yourself, let us say, a Victrola, simply a mechanical conveyor for the music.

Now I never forgot those words, pompous as they sound. I think what he meant by 'ego' was what I would come to call 'psyche'; but I was not wrong to believe in the experience he was describing. It would, over time, emerge as something more radical than he had in mind. Ramon, like your father, was somewhat short on humor, but you had a taste for such melancholy types. They seemed to confirm your own assessment of yourself by their indifference, and in doing so confirmed their own genius in your eyes. If they knew how worthless you were, then they only knew what you knew already, and that insight made them into gods.

I told Ramon I would try to do what he said, and did. We were at that moment about to separate. He gave me a sudden, slight, ingratiating smile and touched my sleeve.

Your friend Honey, he said.

What about her?

She seems to have – eh – expectations – I mean, about me, you know. Tell her if she were four years older perhaps then, yes, but she's a child. You understand.

I nodded and moved on, not liking this shift in his manner nor my role. It was one thing to be a medium for Mozart's music and another to be a medium for Ramon's intentions. But, as you remember, I came to you almost at once to pass on his message. And contrary, I'm sure, to his expectations, you were elated.

I see you in this photograph. It is really what you were. Lying on your stomach on the sand in that blue one-piece bathing suit, your blonde hair in a page-boy, your red lipsticky mouth laughing, your chin up, by your side on the blanket some lotion and a book of French poetry. Utterly conventional, a cute American blonde. You have, for a little while, achieved an exterior that matches your longing to 'pass' for normal. Curled up hair and neat clothes, you were becoming compulsive about showing this image to the world. This must have been sometime, somewhere, that summer.

We all had to spend our energies arranging events so you wouldn't get upset. We had to distract and entertain you so you wouldn't get depressed. And after the way you threw yourself on me that night, to grind out some pleasure, I realized that there were no limits to the demands you made on us, your friends, and your family.

Remember the time I gave you my secret for composing music: to listen to the sounds of the city and the people in it, and to play them, including the radiator or bird-song, to tune to the random car-wind and siren for your inspiration. Already I was breaking loose from convention, but I only told you about this because you were restless, bored, about to have a fit of some kind. I told you in order to settle you down. There are names for this kind of friendship. None of them can grasp the complexity of it. I gave you that secret but didn't dare tell you that Ramon was leaving in June in case it would send you over the edge. You promptly leaned out the window and began jotting down the beat of the sounds and their names.

All the functions of the body should be, I feel, subjected to one goal: work. That is, one should think of eating, sleeping, drinking, shitting, as preceding their object, work. One eats to work. One must not work to eat. The best civilization will understand this. Work brings the same surprising joy that self-abnegation brings. And by work I do not mean labor.

I have stayed with this belief, though you continually proved me wrong. You had instant revelations that you captured and turned into little songs and poems without revision, editing, or doubt. And they were quickly applauded, loved, while I was still huddled over the first draft, thinking.

You told me you also had continual and instant orgasms wherever you went. On the subway, in the classroom, climbing the stairs, sleeping.

Anatomy is destiny is what we were taught. There must be some link between these two qualities of yours!

Anyway, I think of the morning you sat on my bed eager to discuss our summer plans. I would be going for the first time to Europe with Alice and Henry. I assumed you would be going to the usual Cape Cod house. We were already studying for finals and I was preparing for a recital. We hadn't seen much of each other, mostly because of my fanatic attention to my own work. You were whipping along, doing fine, wearing a tidy page-boy haircut and contradictory Beatnik clothes. You were constantly humming new melodies to accompany your poems, or else smoking. And you looked happy a lot, needing me only infrequently as a caretaker.

Now you announced, I have to spend the weekend here.

Okay, but why?

I can't tell.

Tsch.

Just tell Alice I'm staying Friday, though.

Okay, but what about Saturday?

I'll tell you afterwards.

After what?

You sprang up and ran to the door with a casual wave goodbye. Then looked back to say, 'Remember, Mary. You and I. We will be great. Great! No matter what. Our music.'

It's odd, when I think of it, how from the age of ten, a person receives no physical love. Pre-adolescence is a dry area: a desert of sharp shadows, bright light, trees as old as Methuselah, parched streams. No parents haul you onto their knees, wrestle with you, rub their faces against yours, breathe you in as you breathe them. It's all over. Desolation. The craving to be touched remains. Pimples sprout where no kisses rain. Adolescents have nothing but each other for years. Boys will be boys, wrestling under a tree after school, or riding around girls on bikes in circles, making wisecracks. And girls drag through these days, overweight or acne-splotched or mad. Loving touches from a father or a mother would have soothed us, I'm sure. I've seen a couple of happy families in all these years, and in them invariably there is this contact, persisting even through the early teens; but how rare it is.

I remember when you came home from school with me on that Friday you had a little overnight bag in your hand, your book bag over your shoulder. A light shirt-waist dress and red flats. Shaved legs, shaved underarms, washed and curled hair. This was your new clean image in full. I thought of you, not as Venus emerging in a splash from clean radiant saltwater, but as a tragic poet, a nymphet. We watched Sid Caesar and Imogene Coca, stole some sherry, and got smashed. Alice and Henry hid away in their bedroom under glowing lights, the windows open to the spring air and crickets. I knew they took some pleasure in this friendship. They were snobs, and the presence of a bluestocking Boston girl, crazy or not, erased the subtle stain of my illegitimacy. They encouraged your visits, and when we were alone, they never came near us. I think you felt safe with your old shrink nearby, in that quiet house where we could get drunk, revel alone, and whisper all night. It wasn't until the morning of that particular occasion that you began to show signs of anxiety, the ones I had grown used to.

Often I rise at daybreak to see the world clean. Sailors must do the same. Homer and Melville write of it: a consciousness of dawn pervades their language and transforms each observation. Like the bright-woven colors along the edges of medieval manuscripts, each page of their writing has a brilliant rim. It must be the dawn. Hear the early birds sing, seagulls breezing in off Boston Harbor. The gray-gold pallor of aurora. The first sounds of trucks and trolleys humming, workdays beginning, an occasional light in a kitchen window, the orange light of the rising sun on glass. If you have been awake for this, your day is longer; by afternoon you are, like the sun, beginning to sink; but your hours have spears of radiance, burning edges. You are, at least unconsciously, reminded of innocence, its loss.

Shit, you cried on Friday, I can't concentrate.

Well then, let's take a walk.

But the exam!

You'll do okay, don't worry.

So we took a walk to the Esplanade. The edges of the river were muddy from recent rains and a slight smell of gas and fish rose off the brown water. We climbed up into the shell – its huge stage for summer concerts vacant – and hung our legs over the edges, staring across the river at the ugly factory skyline.

About tomorrow, I'm sorry I can't tell you, you said.

Okay, don't.

I will maybe then.

It must have occurred to me that Ramon was involved, but I squelched any thought of him. You wanted to curl your hair again, so we went home, and I watched you through the mirror, how you kept grasping your abdomen and groaning in anticipation. Your face burned. You were up to no good, but I felt no responsibility. If curiosity was pressing, I only know I concealed it, as a matter of pride perhaps, being excluded from the drama, or being used only insofar as I was useful. I didn't want to show, even to myself, how involved I was in your life.

You left for your piano lesson at three o'clock. I read myself to sleep, early. I remember it was a drizzly night. The patter and drill of the raindrops enclosed me in a pleasing isolation. Alice and Henry were out. I felt no fear, but its opposite, in being completely alone. The radio, the rain, and in silence a quiet dialogue (or so it seemed) with the powers that might be. The bed you had slept in on other nights was folded neatly close by.

I woke with a jolt, the edge of my bed sinking under the weight of another body. The room was dark, but I sensed the imminence of daybreak, murder.

Honey, you said.

I knew you though I couldn't see you. My heart was edible, pounding in the roof of my mouth. Damp hair and cold feet. You lay against me, fully dressed.

Why tonight? Why are you here?

Ramon let me in. The basement window, you whispered.

Get in the other bed.

I'm cold.

So you pressed up against me. You were one of those people who cling, who stand close to speak to you, who put their faces only a foot away to make the most mundane announcement, and from whom you withdraw involuntarily at their approach. After the last time at your house, however, I was sickened by your proximity. Too much female!

What happened? I asked stiffly.

Almost everything.

What do you mean?

But we didn't. That's why I'm here. He wouldn't.

I told you I was still tired, I wanted more sleep, I implored you to get in the other bed, but you hung on, cold and tremulous. The dog's bloody ear. You could do anything. I was scared of you.

The light was beginning to pierce the darkness of the room, you were wide awake. We went to a French restaurant and then to this place, and ooohhhh, you whispered.

I can imagine, I said quickly.

No, you can't; you can't possibly.

Well, then, I won't.

I'll tell you, you hissed against my face, let me tell you, I love him! I would have done anything for him and I will.

HER STORY

It is Thursday. They are sitting side by side on the piano bench at the conservatory. The room is empty but for them. She is trying to play a very simple piece by Mozart, when his knee touches hers and she can't handle the keys. She is shaking all over. He puts his hand in her hair and turns her face to look at him. They kiss. He says he can't leave the country until he has made love to her. So they make their plan for Saturday. From three until six they walk around the city, getting his plane ticket and a traveling bag and returning his late books to the library. Then they go to a little French restaurant, where they can sit outside, and she can't eat a bite, so he finishes her plate, and she drinks his wine. They go to his flat near the Fenway, taking the bus to get there. Two rooms. Shabby. Just an old radio for music. He has a bottle of wine for them. They sit on the floor listening to an FM station, drinking wine, and necking. First her breasts – it takes a long time. Then he takes off her dress. They lie on the bed. He is still fully dressed. She wears panties and a bra. He puts his hand down and in, then jumps up and says he can't go on. She begs him to finish, but he won't, and so they just lie beside each other talking and touching, and he tells her how he feels it would be dishonorable to take her virginity just when he is leaving. She unzips him and begs him to do it anyway, but he continues to refuse. Finally they say they will meet in a year in Switzerland when she is finished with school, and he insists on bringing her to Mary's house to sleep out the rest of the night. They have to walk there in the drizzle because the buses have stopped running, and on the way she tells him she will return the next day, for the last time, just to say goodbye.

Gold light sprayed the windows facing east. The rain had stopped; everything was shining wet. I got out of bed to watch the seagulls. I imagined myself free from the place and the hour sailing perhaps to the North Pole, walls of white ice, sculptures gleaming in blue light, with a fur coat for warmth and company. Behind me she rose from the bed and took off her dress. She threw it in a ball on the floor. Graying pink panties and a graying bra, the clean exterior abandoned. I remember I put on my dressing gown at once. Protection.

You'll have to hide here, I told her.

She wasn't listening; she had pushed her hands down inside her panties and was massaging her curls. Rubbing her labia together, it made a soft clicking sound and she crossed her legs like a child impatient to pee, hunching down slightly and grinning at me. The curls gone from her hair, her face was partially shaded by gold.

'Just the thought of his hands,' she said ... 'It's embarrassing, you leave, go, I can't help it, I mean, sometimes sitting on the piano bench beside him, I'd get these ... '

I headed for the door fast while she cried out to me: I'm sorry!

Hesitating then I saw that her eyes held a moist, myopic stare and she rolled back up under the covers, turned to the wall. I left the room and changed into my clothes in the bathroom, ripping at them as if they were made of rubber and elastic, they seemed to snap around me in my anxiety. When I returned to the room, swaddled and sweating, you were still under the covers, but sitting upright and smiling apologetically.

Do you forgive me? You wanted to know.

I'm going downstairs. You can do what you want, was my response.

Don't tell Alice I'm here!

Don't worry.

I wish you were as happy as I am. You're like Jiminy Cricket. I'll buy you some chocolate earrings made of grasshopper legs.

She made me laugh, but I hid it from her, and spoke with my face to the wall.

Let's just pretend that you are coming over here this morning to study. You stay here. Let's just stick with our plan.

Okay, you said cheerfully, and you must have thrown your legs out from under the sheets with your panties hooked to your foot. They floated past me into the wastepaper basket. I know you don't believe me, you said, but I'm leaving with Ramon.

Good. But how? I asked, now glancing in your direction.

I have a passport, you said, and I'll get money out of my father's desk.

Your yellow hair was sticking up like straw, the morning sun glowing on your brow. A confidential smile, lower lip engaged to upper teeth, lips upwardly curling, and a post-coital blush: you were at your prettiest.

But Ramon, I said, he won't want you.

Wait and see.

I shrugged and turned, hearing the sounds of Alice and Henry wakening. Water running, a toilet.

You hide in here, I told you, I'll be back.

(Now, looking back through the years I realize that the problem of luck is at the heart of our efforts. Some people are blessed, some people struggle for small blessings, and some struggle and are never blessed. All can have moments of intense happiness. To those who have, more shall be given. Yet they fear this luck. Like Honey they pray: let my children be ordinary that they may not suffer from luck. They believe that suffering is a punishment for getting something without working for it. Yet most of the suffering souls are the anonymous many who have had to obey the law in order to avoid a head-on, ruinous collision with fate. You will not see their names in any award book.)

Alice sat up in her bed, a heap of pillows supporting her back and head. On Sunday mornings Henry always brought her breakfast in bed – the Sunday paper would follow – and he sat in his bed sipping coffee and reading the news. Pale light seeped through the heavy white drapery covering two bow windows in the room. A soft blue rug and the glow of her polished bureau and dressing table always gave the room a special warmth. Yet I felt awkward there. The odor of sleep and their particular body smells hung in the morning light; and I hung at the door, looking in, not wanting to cross the threshold into this secular ritual.

Come on in, darling.

Oh that's okay.

You look tired. Studying?

Yeah.

Go down and have some breakfast. I started to go, then turned.

Honey is coming over soon.

Oh?

She needs some help with history.

Fine, but remember this afternoon.

I will.

I didn't and don't like to lie. I become my own enemy with traps lying around my brain. One should at least state the facts, with respect to nature, in order to ensure the continuance of order. Alice lit a cigarette and the blue veil concealed her expression.

You mustn't study too hard, she said.

I won't.

Summer is almost here.

She watched me closely but I looked off and away till the objects around me became shadows I could pass through. A temporary sleep washed through my system. It happens all the time, even now. People notice it, this passing inattention, stasis.

Well, you must be hungry, she said.

Down in the kitchen I felt better. Henry was there, put-ting together a tray of coffee, rolls and butter, jam, and boiled eggs. Everything in that house was orderly and rich. The silverware was real silver, polished by the maid, the counters white and gleaming, pots and pans all in a row. This tidiness was provided by others but it gave me a familiarity with elegance I would never be able to shake. Culture stacked along the walls, no dust.

Henry automatically cleaned up after himself, sweeping crumbs into the palm of his hand, and ran a cloth after them. Bound in a plaid bathrobe and unshaven, he looked old to me, a grandfather. He had these mild vague eyes that required kindness from others.

Do you want my egg? he asked.

I'll do my own.

I can wait. Have it.

No, no, please.

It's warm out, he remarked.

I opened the back door to the sweet May air: moist pink magnolia blossoms and a row of yellow tulips, stiff as wax.

Honey's coming over, I told him.

He went upstairs. I waited a few minutes before I climbed the carpeted stairs on tiptoes. On the left at the head of the stairs was Alice's room, the door partly ajar. I crept along the edges of each step to avoid making creaking sounds, but their voices sounded very close, though low in tone, and my heart was thumping. My silence made it necessary for me to hear them, although I didn't want to.

It must be her solitariness, said Alice. She's bound to show some sort of symptoms. Talking to herself, well, it's not such a big thing, is it?

Her dish ran away with her spoon. She grabbed them before they could slide off the tray and I heard the clink of silver on china.

I think it's more serious than that, said Henry. I always wonder when her early childhood traumas will begin to manifest themselves.

Alice gave a toasty laugh. Beware you don't bring them on, she told him, by anticipating them. Henry didn't comment. I heard the newspaper land on the front steps outside with a thump. My skin, already crawling, turned cold. I didn't dare go up or down. Trapped in a position of deceit, I hated them and myself.

Ah well, sighed Alice, I won't worry about it. Mary is a good girl. But maybe she needs a break from us this summer.

How and when? said Henry.

We could go to Europe alone and leave her here with someone.

Perhaps Lotte would take her for awhile, said Henry.

Now that's a thought!

Let me go get the paper, he said.

But do you think it will be all right? asked Alice.

I think so. I agree she needs a break from us.

And, really, in a way, from Honey too. It's too intense.

I flew down the stairs and into the little bathroom beside their patients' waiting room. I locked myself in. Now, shivering all over, I didn't wish I had never heard their conversation, but, on the contrary, showered the air with a mysterious series of thanks, because I realized: They could live without me!

When I finally joined you upstairs, continuing the deceit for everyone's sake, I didn't tell you what I had over-heard or felt. Instead I got dressed and said I wanted to go to your house for breakfast.

Okay. I can pack and get the money there, you said.

So we glided down the stairs and out. The special texture of the spring air, the quiet streets, and the soft benevolent flowering contrasted so greatly with each of our dark and chaotic centers. I am amazed, now, at how well we performed, pretending we were simple and gay like the spring, as jocund as the jonquils that bordered our walk. For that short time I understood how you could be so wild, how extreme emotion can lead to extreme acts. You, of course, thought that I had finally entered your imagination, that I was excited by your fantasy of Ramon. It didn't occur to you that I might have passions of my own, but I felt released from the bondage of Alice and Henry who didn't need me as much as I had believed. They were right. I did need a little time off from them and them from me.

We sat in your kitchen and consumed heaps of toast, circled by bottles of liquor, dirty dishes, ground-out cigarette butts and old cat food. You tossed back your hair and grinned crumbs at me. Everyone was still sleeping here. The dirty clothes piled in a corner of the upstairs hall looked like another body. I expected as much, your mother perhaps. We got convulsed with giggles and rolled around your room.

Soon you were packing and I was watching, the old dread and sobriety beginning to return. Your excitement didn't lapse for a minute; it made you daring. You went to your father's desk, while I stayed behind, and returned with your passport and an envelope full of cash.

Where will we go now? I asked.

To Ramon.

Are you sure?

Of course!

We had to hurry before the house awakened. I was increasingly fearful, but the good May air restored my spirits slightly. It reminded me of being happy and that was better than nothing. On the hem of my mind the irritating tug of freedom, like a wind off the sea, began to make itself felt. I had often felt a desire to be elsewhere, but I had never followed it out. If you have ever lain in the dark, before sleep, listening, straining to hear the farthest sound, you will understand the direction I was taking. There were sounds out there I could actually hear, available to my ear, my consciousness, though I couldn't see their source. But I would! I would travel, I would escape. I would know the price of every room, experience and emotion, if it broke me. I looked at you breathing beside me. Your sudden lust in the morning came back to me, and I blushed. I wondered if I would ever have physical desires like those. Parasols drooped over us, unsprung buds, pale green. A mist of morning air draped the distance, our destination. It dawned on me that Ramon was your victim, your prey.

Poor Ramon, he might not like this, I said.

He'll love it.

You gave me a quick snapping-turtle glance. Your hair blew over your face. And we turned down the narrow street near the Fenway, where he lived. It was an ordinary brick building for students. Small windows facing other small windows across the street. The sun was approaching ten.

Here we are, you said.

Good luck.

Don't tell a soul.

I won't.

So you went in and I went on, back the way we had come.

I imagined I would see you again soon, or if I didn't it would be because you had killed yourself or been dragged into a mental hospital. I was trying to be realistic, not guilty. I was trying to distance myself from the catastrophe that always followed disappointment for you. And I was trying to hold on to my own little piece of pleasure, a few weeks of freedom in summer.

At home Alice and Henry acted as if they didn't know I had gone out at all, and I didn't say otherwise, and this way we were conspirators in our own lack of responsibility for each other.

It was our custom to have a late lunch on Sundays with my grandmother – Henry's mother, that is – in Sudbury. She lived in a nineteenth-century wooden house with two gables and long windows. It stood off the road on six acres of land, and seemed to me, always, a haunted house. Hardwood floors, oriental rugs, heavy dark curtains, and the damp smell of a country house. Most spooky of all were the somber portraits of dead members of the Casement family, dating back into the eighteenth century. Henry's mother was in her nineties. We called her Baba.

This was the relic of a mother: a crumpled white figure, a piece of white paper. Freckled hands shone like pearl, the neck was as checkered as sunlight on screens. Really, just a skeleton in skin; yet she dressed in fine dark silks with real jewels at her throat and on her fingers, she was elegant and intelligent. She listened to the news twice a day and used the Talking Books series on her phonograph to keep up with novels. A faint smell of Chanel lay in her tiny soft cheek where I kissed her and her tiny brown eyes darted under reptilian lids. A little deaf, a little blind, she was on the whole in good health. Her circulation was her main complaint – ironically, for she was obsessed by blood. *Water to water, blood to blood*, she would say. *Blood always returns to blood.* No matter how much she liked you, if you were not 'blood', she disposed of you swiftly at the slightest slip in behavior. (She had, it was said, been devoted to Henry's sister-in-law until that woman divorced her son; then she stopped all communication with her for good even though there were children.) I sensed that she didn't accept me because I was not, by blood, attached. Yet she always sent me a check on birthdays, Christmas, Easter. Little cards, presents – bought, never her own books or jewelry which she gave to my cousins.

She would not give me anything that belonged to the family though she was the soul of good manners and grace toward me. She was fascinating to me; I longed to win her over. The ritual of her life and behavior was exotic in that it bore no relation to the outside world. I had to respect her for this rigidity, being unable to respect her for anything else.

I was always given the task of reading aloud to her after lunch. On the big family lunches, when her other grandchildren were there, I was the only one who was required to stay indoors after lunch and help out.

It's a privilege, Alice said. It shows how much she admires you, Mary.

I assented to this explanation, understanding that I must not force Alice and Henry to take sides with me against Baba. It would be dangerous for me and painful for them. But I was fully conscious of my Cinderella role.

This particular Sunday was, of course, more difficult than usual. I couldn't get Honey and Ramon off my mind, I kept looking at the clock. I didn't want to eat. Finally, after dessert, Baba spoke.

Mary, come to my room, dear.

Read to you?

No. Today let's have a little chat, just the two of us.

The last thing I wanted! But she took up her two canes and I had to follow her up the padded staircase to her bedroom: a canopy bed, oak-caned dresser, oak-carved desk, gold-gilt mirror, and a huge armchair. She lay down on the bed and I covered her with her quilt. Lying down she looked frail and broken, but her bright and willful eyes pierced me. I sat down.

What's all the fuss about? she snapped.

What fuss?

Don't be sullen, my dear, it doesn't at all suit you. You must try to be clear of face and clear of heart. You're too bosomy for sullen looks. Try to avoid making too many expressions or your face will wrinkle prematurely. You're too full of expression. This won't do you any good, none at all, in the world of men. My mother told me to keep my eyebrows and the corners of my lips smooth at all times. She said it would secure my youth and hide my feelings. A fine bit of advice, I never forgot it, and look at that portrait, there, of myself as a young woman. How old would you say I am?

I looked at the picture. I had looked at it many, many times before, trying to find traces of the young in the old or the old in the young. Dark-haired, long-necked, dark velvet dress, hands folded on her lap, her lips pursed slightly, her eyebrows arched, a conventional beauty. There was a certain worldly attitude there. I guessed twenty-one.

No, my dear Mary, thirty-five.

Wow.

Not when you realize how carefully I worked to achieve that clear skin ... Oh well now, the main thing is you could have a tendency to flesh, almost peasant one would think, and you must not increase the expression of foreign intelligence, an absence of style, by letting your face reveal everything. No. It's imperative you remember this if you want to marry well. You have been very lucky so far, as you know. Don't ruin it with any-thing so superficial as a look. You're a good, honest girl, good with your hands, salt of the earth, poor –

She went to sleep abruptly. A snore as sharp as a fart sprang from her lips. Her mouth dropped open. A dark hole. Death stood over her, watching her chest rise and fall under the quilt and I felt the forgiveness it is so easy to feel toward a person sleeping. I wanted to pick up the phone beside her bed and call Honey's house, but I was too scared of being caught doing so – and, instead, I went down to Alice and Henry in the dark living room. They were at the window together, looking out, when I came in.

She fell asleep, I told them.

I think we'll go home then.

I have homework, my exams.

We left. Two maids were constantly on duty. The old lady was safe from almost every surprise. For a while.

The scandal hit the scene hard and fast. I couldn't believe what happened, having expected you to be rejected and to slash your wrists or drink gas or simply run mad through the streets of Boston. But no. You and Ramon flew off together to Switzerland. I was cross-examined many times by school officials, even the police, but I pretended I knew nothing. Henry made me slip, a week later, in a small detail, and his eyes and mine locked. He turned the key with his kindness, so to speak, and never told anyone, not even me, that he knew that I knew everything about you and Ramon from the beginning.

His silence was a bond between us in those last days before summer. The other people accepted my story because I had a history of good behavior and honesty. It took a couple of weeks before they could track you down. When they did, your father flew over after you, but didn't return with you; instead he helped arrange your marriage and returned to Boston alone.

In the summer I got your letter from the Italian Riviera. Photograph included: Sixteen and *tutti contenti*. Marriages like that sometimes last, Henry remarked. This one won't, said sensible Alice. Now I wished that they would take me to Europe with them after all; I prayed that I would see you soon. But in the middle of June, they told me they had to fly to Europe alone – 'We have a boring conference we have to attend' – and they were sending me to Cape Cod to stay with Lotte Lett.

Just for three weeks, dear. Then we'll all go to Quebec.

I wanted to see Honey, I started to say, but held in my words so they wouldn't feel guilty. They looked distressed anyway. The three of us were at the dinner table, a quartet of candles burning in the center. The early summer breezes damp on the screens. I started to rise, to rush to the kitchen to hide the contortions on my face, the urge to cry out, but Henry awkwardly got up, passed behind my chair, leaned over and planted a dry kiss on my forehead.

That's my girl, he said.

It was such an unusual gesture of affection coming from him, that it took all my self-control to keep from bursting into tears. I remember thinking that Baba would be proud of me under the circumstances, and I went into the kitchen to do the dishes, without letting them know what I felt.

I will never understand why certain events in my life served to save me from disaster since I never did anything to deserve it. I was a child of war and cold war and lived in a state of sublimated dread. I expected the worst to happen most of the time. Maybe it already had happened. In any case I had learned a combination of discipline and evasion that worked well for many years of my youth. Something was bound to interrupt that.

The point is, a terrible airplane wreck wrenched Alice and Henry from my life that summer. I could have been with them, but I was not. Instead I was with Lotte when it happened. Lotte was a lawyer who lived on the Cape year round. A horsey face and tall body, short white hair. She was Alice's oldest friend; they grew up together in the Midwest and were important to each other, having struggled for their educations together.

Although she did not come from that region, Lotte was the epitome of a certain kind of New England Protestant woman – country tweeds, hearty, frank but incapable of expressing affection. She never married. She involved herself in liberal causes and was thoroughly committed to her work. I liked and trusted her though she was intimidating and brusque. She expected me to be self-sufficient and high-minded. She was shocked, I remember, on finding me reading *Modern Romances* and *My True Story*, popping bubble gum – I, the product of Alice and Henry.

The night the phone call came we had just returned from an outdoor lobster dinner with friends of hers. I was on my way to bed, when Henry's brother phoned. He told her about the crash off the coast of Ireland and asked Lotte to tell me what had happened; we didn't hear from him again until the Memorial Service – 'a small family affair' – was over. The three days are just one more hole in time for me. I remember wishing I could cry. I had a picture of you, Honey, beside my bed, and a picture of Alice and Henry together, along with a few of the letters they had sent me. I know I put all of these away in my suitcase, out of sight, quite quickly. Lotte, as I say, was incapable of expressing affection, but I knew, instinctively, that she would become my legal guardian and see to it that I continued with school and piano in a style I was accustomed to enjoying. She was, of course, stunned by the news, and hiding her grief under a mask of false resignation didn't help. We couldn't communicate our shock and sorrow to each other at all.

It was only after the extraordinary phone call from Henry's brother, when he mentioned the Memorial Service and told Lotte what the arrangements were to be regarding my future, that she broke down and spoke to me as an equal.

You must realize that these people are terrible! she cried, grasping the edge of the kitchen table. They've always been the lowest form of snobs. Always. And I have to tell you that Alice and Henry were not free from them. I warned them, and now look. Your name was never included in their Will: they were cowards. But this is the limit. You weren't even asked to the service. I will never understand them, never.

Then she left the kitchen, and I didn't get a chance to ask for details. Instead I remember I wore one of those grotesque smiles the face assumes in response to bad news; it's a kind of proof that the body is a costume in its own lonely parade. No matter how hard the features try to wear the appropriate emotions, they can be duped. It was physically impossible for me to pursue Lotte into the depths of the house asking for answers to my questions while my horror had not caught up to my expression. I realized nobody on earth loved me. Therefore, I did not exist.

Two days later there was a hurricane. I mean, incredible as it may sound, too Gothic for words, the imminent presence of this hurricane swung over and after Lotte's revelation to me. She was, I know, busy on the phone making arrangements regarding my future some of the time; the rest of the time, she kept me busy down at the Boat Club where people were preparing for the storm. There was a wild and unexpected camaraderie building up alongside the storm in the strange phenomenon of joy that precedes disaster. It's as if people are so relieved at the possibility of obliteration that they would be disappointed if harm was averted completely. I mean, worried as they were about the fate of their possessions – mainly spiffy little sailboats – there was a contradictory undercurrent of longing that all should be lost. A chance to start from scratch? Without lifting a hand? Sometimes a husband prays that his wife will die, so he will lose her and win sympathy at the same time. Similarly the hurricane seemed to offer these affluent folks a second chance at greed. There was much talk about what kind of boat they would buy if the old one was demolished.

The hurricane hit around noon. First a humid stillness dripped from the sky, then the wind rose by degrees, bringing down rain and broken branches. No birds. The wind roared like the pink and yellow interior of a shell, a hollow sound, the splashing rain barely audible under the wind. Things broke. The havoc attracted me in my already disturbed state. Being young I still imagined nature arranged itself around my need for drama. I felt the hurricane had been sent to me, to free me like a branch off a tree, to send me spinning. To weep with me. Nothing could keep me in. So I went out clutching my wallet, my identity.

I pushed against the wet wind and the scrubby Cape Cod underbrush. Blueberry, poison ivy, sea grass, slashed my ankles. I had to close my eyes. The air was solid as a balloon. I had to roll it ahead of me, clutching my bag against me. Heading for the beach. No big trees to knock me flat, just this lowdown seascape, whirling sand and soaking rain.

The sea was tremendous: voluminous breakers, higher than me, whacked on the sand and rolled the width of the beach. I watched from the top of a dune. The sky had a damaged appearance, ripped veils, violence, reflected in blue, bruised water. It was more like winter, crumpled monuments of snow, the jaws of the whale, skeletal interior, forbidding. Yet the air was terribly hot; the drops of rain were warm as bathwater.

With my face drenched, my thoughts were not clear. But I hurried over the dunes toward the town, shoving the balloon or being shoved and knocked down by it, depending which way I went. At one point I was thrown down, where I remained curled into a ball, while the wind pushed down on my head and sand blinded me. I was halfway between beach and town, and felt as if I were disconnected from all geography and was, like a speck of dust, afloat in a world without names. At first it was a dreadful feeling. My bowels turned to water. I couldn't see. I thought of Lotte's kindly horselike face, big nose, melancholy eyes. I can go back to her, I told myself, and she will take care of me. We will pretend we are somehow related; we will pretend destiny designed all these losses around our union. But I couldn't do it. Why? I must have been crazy. Was it because you had left the country, were gone? I remember feeling an abject stoop-shouldered gratitude, or guilt, when I was with Lotte. It was not much different from what I felt with Alice and Henry, but it was worse. This would be the way I would feel always if I returned to her house, and I couldn't.

I had to move. My bowels were raging, so I crawled along the sand, my bag in my hand, my arms getting slashed by the grass, until I had to stop and crouch in the rain and wind and grass to shit. A complete renunciation of my body to the world. Pains, and a good purged feeling as I crawled away, aware that I was giving birth, and talking to God the whole time. Face to the wind, I actually came up with a new name for myself and with that self-annihilating act I birthed myself alone and again. With this act I joined my generation.

Late that night I passed through Boston on the bus, with my wallet still in my dungaree pocket, damp clothes, and a new name. Everyone was talking about the hurricane and the roads were littered with branches and leaves. I think I felt like Jesus entering Jerusalem with palms cast down in His path. I felt good. I had to change in Boston for a bus to New York, and I did so in a wild state of excitement. Reborn! Disconnected from everyone, every place, I had the fearlessness of a maniac. It seemed I was doing what I had always longed to do, what I was born to do.

The route to New York was familiar. With Alice and Henry I had been there, traveling down through Hartford and New Haven. The city, in the mist of summer and the brilliant clarity of a day after storms, was showered in the light of dawn. Black shadows spread like rugs across the streets, watery gutters, papers wrapped around poles, smells of baking and gasoline. We rolled into the bus terminal, and my stomach rolled over. I had nowhere to go.

I stepped into the belly of the city with only a nightgown and a toothbrush rolled up in my bag and two-hundred-and-ten dollars cash in my pocket. This was the money Alice and Henry had given me for spending over the summer. It was 6:35 a.m. The temperature was 70°. The streets, newly washed by rain, shone around me. I was sixteen years old and ignorant. And I think I was saved from despair by the presence of a friend – you! – to whom I could write it all. I thought all the time of what I would say in my letters, how I would describe each scene to you, and this plan gave me courage. Your distant presence supplied a constant purpose for my acts and fed the spirit of revolt.

I stepped back into the terminal where the name *San Francisco* was being called aloud. I took this to be a Voice for me. What else could I do?

(Be Honey as Heidi, leaping through Alpine meadows, spring green, mountainous aerial views of white and purple flowers, rivulets rushing down towards a glassy ravine. I try to follow, but I am a rock, the first female ever carved in stone.)

When I wake up, in motion, the bus is cutting across a gray American landscape on a strip of darker gray.

This was not a happy journey. I was racked with coughs, a sore chest, chills, and fear. I stared out the bus window, keeping my coat on the seat beside me, hoping that no one would sit beside me. My anonymity was complete, but it drove me to desire nothing more than isolation. If I should have to speak, I would scream. Every four hours the bus stopped and we got out at a roadside restaurant; but I avoided the other passengers all the way. Each time I slipped into a phone booth and looked up the name CASEMENT.

On the bus I curled near the window and coughed, sucking hard candies, watching us move into dusk and darkness. The bus filled up. I knew I would lose my privacy and considered getting off in Omaha, before it was too late, and just living there. The windowpane was cold, patches of snow lay in the darkness, layers of vaults unlocked inside me, echoing sounds, jerking me back and forth between sleep and no sleep.

When we stopped, I hurried through the dark frost to the warmth of the rest place. I went to the phone booth first and found three Casements listed. Then to the Ladies Room to wash with the other women. Tea and donuts. I sat on the stool and in the mirror saw the new man or boy down the row of faces, a huge instrument (a cello?) wrapped in black and leaning beside him. He was talking to the fat man beside him, and smoking. His ability to be friendly sickened me. I hated him. He would probably chatter with everyone from here to San Francisco.

The bus was still full so there was no escape from him and I saw him sticking his instrument carefully between the back seat and the rear wall of the bus. Everyone was being very talkative now, over newspapers and smokes, telling each other their life histories, destinations, etc. The dawn light was brightening outside over a pale snowy flatland. Blackbirds flew up from a single tree. He sat down beside me.

This is the best time of day, he said. The most mystical.

Yeah, it's nice.

He has a curled-up copy of *Crime and Punishment* on his knee.

Where are you going? he asked.

San Francisco.

Me too, or anyway to Berkeley.

Is that a cello? I asked politely.

No, bass.

Maybe if I let him know how educated I am, he would leave me alone. He would think I was boring. I decided to tell him that I played the piano quite seriously.

You better see a doctor with that cough, he said first.

I don't know any doctors.

You've never been west before?

No, never, I confessed.

Well, your friends will know one.

I don't have any friends there, I told him.

Why are you going there then?

Don't ask me, I don't know.

He raised his eyebrows and gave me a funny look.

Running away from home?

I don't have any home, I said.

You sound like me.

He laughed and nudged me.

This must be Fate, he said. Two orphans in a storm.

I didn't know what to think, he was looking me over, appraising me with an arch and curly expression. He thought I was funny; something about me made him laugh. I wiped my nose and ran my tongue across my teeth: was something awful showing? But when I glanced at his face, I saw he was generally amused, ready for a laugh. I was not the center of the joke.

And he did, indeed, laugh and talk a lot. He was one of these people who never seem to hear what you say, but, later, will throw back your smallest remark, imprinting it with his own thoughts and interpretations. His name was Heaven. His mother's name was Celeste but she was not a home to him. He was traveling to San Francisco in order to get into the jazz scene. He wanted to play with a group out there.

I'm a complete escapist. I always seek the geo-graphical cure and it always works, he tells me. When you are down and out, leave town. Never believe a word of pop psychology. It will ruin your chances at happiness, freedom.

I feel guilty all the time, I told him.

You probably *should* feel guilty. I'm sure you have *plenty* of good reasons for that. We all do. We're all very bad.

I ended up settling in and telling him everything about you, Ramon, and my own early childhood. What a relief!

He was delighted by my tale. He actually stopped talking to listen and wanted every detail of the hurricane, your family, Lotte, Baba, what you and Ramon looked like, and so on. I told him, at first, in a quavering emotional voice, but he egged me on to see it all in a more extreme light.

Now you must *not* write to Honey, telling her where you are, because that will ruin everything. She will tell, she's a hysteric. Information like this will incite her to cry it out in the streets so she can get the attention for having it. I know her type. Watch out! If you really want your freedom, that is. And you must begin to see her as a metaphor for something else in your soul. Don't keep relentlessly repeating the details about Honey to yourself and anyone else who cares to listen. The details aren't the point, for you. The configuration is. What does she *mean* to you?

After this outburst of advice, he gave me more and more until he was ready to talk about himself again. There was, I could see, a consistent attitude buried in his chatter. He was a Beatnik, a critical outsider, he was impatient with pomposity and believed in religious thought, the power of the brain to reach God. (He gave me a long speech on Eckhart, Augustine, Aquinas, Kerouac, Kierkegaard, and Sufism.)

If someone can't make me laugh in person I won't have anything to do with them, he said. But I like these heavy cats anyway, the big thinkers. You look like a big thinker but you are funny without knowing it.

So we traveled on westward.

What do you think I am? he asked me.

What do you mean?

Rich man, poor man, white man or black?

I don't know.

I'm all four. And maybe not a man at all. You don't believe me, but it's the *truth*. Amazing grace, it's the *truth*. *My* father was poor and black, my mother was rich and white. Now she is not rich at all, she spent it all gambling. Poor Celeste. She was a math whiz. It's where I got my music skills.

In the night he said to me before turning his head towards sleep:

The saddest part of your story belongs to your adoptive parents. They make me much sadder than you do. Their fate, their fate.

I couldn't let his insight take root in me.

After all, we had had a happy day and night, and he had a wine-sack we shared in the dark. My cough came and went. I was discovering America. I was a pilgrim, an exile, a bird and a bus. I was trying to find out if I existed at all. If you've ever been there before, you will know what it is to be desperate, homeless. If you find kindness, you follow it. So it was with me then. When Heaven left my side to go to the bathroom I panicked that he would not come back. I slept well and deeply that night because he was beside me. If he stayed in the men's room at the restaurant too long, I would know he had deserted me for good. And what would happen at the end of this journey? I knew he would, then, really leave, and I would be nobody.

In the morning the bus climbed out of Reno into the Sierra. The sky was a brilliant blue, the pine trees emerald. As we passed Lake Tahoe, I felt I had smashed though the hoop, a lion. I had gotten to the other side; I was home free. But it was a mixed blessing. The next time the motion of the bus stopped and I got off, that would be the end of being nowhere. I would not tell Heaven how scared I was for fear he would laugh at me. Although I trusted him, I was still my usual self, afraid to impose on anyone for too long. I started to cough.

We'll get you to a doctor first thing, he said.

And that remark, so slight in itself, opened into Paradise for me. He wasn't going to leave me.

HEAVEN

I am in the train. He is in the car traveling beside the train. I am looking at him. He is looking at me. Scraps of countryside glitter between us. Discarded toys and cars. He is driving his car without looking, so I am the safer one, but only in that sense. For I am surrounded by people and activity: Paul is giving Ann three apples and Ann is passing two of them on to Joan who has just received eight from Mrs Monahan and now she has none. She who? How many apples does Joan have? That is, how many apples does Joan have in relation to the distance and the speed traveled by Heaven in the car between point A (when Ann passed two apples to Joan) and point B (when Mrs Monahan discovered she had none.) I am looking out my window at Heaven and trying to solve the impossible question, because I understand that certain events occur exactly in proportion to the passage of light and time; and I also understand how the phone begins to ring in a dream before the real phone begins to ring outside the dream, in the other room, awakening one; and the two issues are related, but I don't know how. Heaven does, but I can't ask him why poor Mrs Monahan has no apples, when others have plenty, no matter how many. Oh Heaven, if your car swerves and loses pace with the train, what will be left of my apple-red heart poisoned daily. The exact moment at which a face and a voice assume an expression of injury, permanent, is the exact moment at which they have ripened.

The wounds in faces. Age. Oh Heaven, I am in love. This is mortal love. My veins are steaming in the heat of your body by mine. Sun heals, so do you, brother. Kindness and confidence: the two ingredients for internal joy. The curls springing from your skull electrify my fingertips. Why are you so *kind*. Why are you so kind. Why are you *so* kind. Why are *you* so kind. Why *are* you so kind. Waving your hand from your car, I tap on the pane of the train. Rattle rattle thump thump. Music curls in the sun between us, tendrils of sound and now the trees flash up between our windows, growth green florid, we will be split by these passages, speed and time for separation, and by the political language growing up around us.

It is hard, or impossible, to recall what occurred in those first days in Berkeley. We took a cab over the Bay Bridge together. I remember that. And some doctor's office: walking pneumonia and penicillin. Heaven must have been around most of that time, because otherwise I wouldn't have known what to do with myself. Yet I do know that he didn't come to Eloise's house with me. He found it for me and pointed the way. I must have been moving around in a state of complete dislocation, being both uprooted and sick. Like a bird on the wing; thanks to him, I somehow landed. My room was at the top of an old brown house just off Telegraph Avenue. I reached it by an outside staircase, wooden, passing one landing into another room occupied by a barber. I had a little bathroom of my own with a shower, the bedroom was yellow and stuffy, a narrow hard bed and a small bureau. A window looked into the leaves of a eucalyptus tree. It was mine. Exactly proportioned to my needs, fifteen dollars a week. The woman who owned the house was a divorcee, Eloise Barnes, who wore trousers and smocks, and did accounting at home for a couple of small companies. She was a complex woman with whom all her boarders became involved. We were her children, her confidantes whom she exploited for company. Fat, generous, blonde, chain-smoking Camels, she would sit with her thin knees spread, a glass of something always on her knees. She reminded me of Honey's mother.

I love people, she would say.

But she was inconsistent; jealous or compassionate, according to her mood. A type I have encountered many times since, and recognize at once. Over the years I have been drawn to these women, the closest things to mothers I have ever known, first for their warmth and welcome, and then for their self-sufficiency, their pleasure in pleasure, their harsh and nihilistic advice.

So I settled in. Sixteen years old, though everyone but Heaven believed I was eighteen. I fell in love with the landscape, its color and space and freedom from all associations. Even the sky was new, higher, less oppressive, not to mention the trees and flowers, the lumpy groundswells giving quick views of the Bay and San Francisco. I had enough cash at first to lay about with, and I recovered my health quickly. Eloise drew me down to her kitchen for soup and fruit. She did crossword puzzles with a glass of whiskey on her knee.

For a time Heaven vanished and I languished, convinced he was gone for good. But then he called and I met him in a loft down by the wharves in San Francisco, where he was camping out among some other musicians. He was in A Mood, as we called it, evasive, druggy and fey. You must expect *nothing* and accept *everything* of me, he said. We are spiritual sisters, we can't be divorced by time or distance, I won't *desert* you. He was smoking hash through an elegant hookah. I didn't like him that way.

So I went home and counted my dwindling money. I would have to get a job, but had no Social Security number and no identification like a birth certificate, to get it with. Fear stalled me. I could not tell Eloise the truth about my condition, for she was conservative (a patriot) in her way, and I feared she might kick me out for lying. I had told her I was from New York City, my name was Bronte Wilde, and I was the only child of an indifferent violinist. My mother had suicided, I said. She pitied me for these details, it would be a terrible insult to her to reveal I had lied.

What are you doing for money? she asked anyway.

Running out.

Well, you better get yourself a job.

How do I get Social Security?

Oh I can't remember, it's been so long. A smart girl like you should be going to College. This is what I don't understand about you East Coast people. You feel so pleased with yourselves. You refuse to go the ordinary route. Why don't you go to school?

I told her I wanted to be a musician, like my father, but a pianist, and I would need money to pay for lessons. So I wanted a job first. She musingly dragged on her cigarette and said she had an idea.

Eloise will take care of you, she said comfortingly. And she did.

(Speaking of types of people, I will tell you which one I am: the drifter at social gatherings, who seems to be no one's close friend. I see, on occasion, others like me, who serve, who are counted on to organize glasses, empty ashtrays, wipe up vomit, who are asked when the fun is over, what we thought of it all. Our opinion is highly valued. Yet no one comes near us; and we are not disagreeable. In literature Jane Eyre would be our model. Too critical, perhaps, for the fun, but not judging. We actually like the position of outsider. We are happy. We know we are necessary. This is how it all works.)

Five years elapsed. From sixteen to twenty-one I lived in that house and worked as a clerk/accountant for a charcoal bricket company in Richmond. Bronte was my name, lying was my game. (It was Heaven who produced, mysteriously, a Social Security card with my name on it after Eloise had found me the job.) I took the bus at seven-thirty each morning and spent my days over a yellowing ledger book, or filing bills, or writing up bills of lading. The company was down on the water near the tracks. The lunch wagon came three times a day, and I stood around outside with the other workers, listening to their banter.

Under the blue and white skies with the others, sipping coffee and eating Danish I felt safe and brave. When I was about seventeen Heaven spoke to me in a steamy coffee shop on Telegraph Avenue. As usual he read my mind, my unspoken question and said something like this.

A happy marriage is the most desirable goal in life and the least possible to achieve. It's all luck and it's all attitude. It's unmistakable when you see it, if you ever do. Believe it or not, I dream of this for myself, a round table, a circle of children, myself cooking and brushing crumbs into the palm of my hand, while a woman, who is my best friend in the world, sits at a piano accompanying me. To be happily married, though, you can't be married already – to your work the way I am.

I started crying and he said *oohhhh* in a very tender and maternal way, drawing me to him.

We'll see, he sighed, we'll see, maybe something new will happen to us.

I will marry my work too. Then we can each have two marriages.

This is exactly what you should do! he cried out. Music! Write!

Then he vanished again for a very long time and I missed him for all of it.

I was walking up the back steps to my room one evening, when I dropped my keys down to the ground below. I cursed and started back down, when the barber's door opened beside me.

What's up, he said.

Oh nothing.

Tea?

Tea?

A cup, with me?

I shrugged okay but first galloped down and up the stairs for the keys. He waited inside his room, a little pot of water boiling up on the hot plate beside his sink. His room smelled of after-shave lotion. It was green and plain. I sat in the only chair there.

You're a barber.

That's right, while I'm a student.

He looked like a priest or a thief. A character from Genet. I always referred to him as The Barber to Eloise who knew him very well and spoke of him as others speak of dogs.

He's clean. No trouble. And quiet, it's good knowing he's around.

He had surprisingly thick arms, I noted, veiny and muscular, tapering into thick but graceful hands. His clothes were tight and shiny.

What kind of student? I asked him.

Hotel Management.

I didn't know that.

I took a cup of tea and he sat on the edge of his bed and stared at me till I felt uneasy.

What? I asked.

Your hair.

What about it?

I'd like to shape it for you.

Really? I blushed.

You could use a good bob cut and conditioning.

At the barber shop?

No, here, I mean, downstairs. Eloise has equipment.

Thank you!

I was thrilled to have him take an interest in my looks since I never did myself. In fact, I had no idea what I looked like. I only sensed a certain chaos from the inside looking out. My face felt like a blotter. Now I hoped I would be tidied up, changed. Eloise was in her usual position at the kitchen table with a drink and the paper; she was glad to see us. On went the lights and Rudolph was given a drink. Eloise got her spray and a towel and a pair of kitchen shears, and a comb. I was placed, head over, at the sink, while she chatted about real estate and Rudolph got to work on me. He had brought down his special shampoo and conditioner. He ran hot water into my hair and poured on the lather. His fingers massaged my skull, while he listened to Eloise and made the appropriate noises for a response. I had never had this experience in my life before, someone else's hands in my hair and the slippery suds under a stranger's fingers. (In those days only adult women went to hairdressers. The mothers cut their daughters' hair, or friends did, or they chopped at it themselves.) He sprayed away the soap, and repeated the lather again, taking his time, his thigh pressed against mine. I became conscious, slowly, of that pressure, but, as I did, I lost touch with the pleasure in my hair. Should I move away? He might get mad or his feelings might be hurt; yet I wanted no contact with his body, even if it were accidental. He lingered over the second rinse, but I knew the end was in sight so I remained motionless, waiting it out.

You have glorious hair, he said, thick as if it was hiding curls inside. You are really letting it go, though. Are you from the Middle East maybe or Spain? It has that luxuriant quality.

I didn't answer directly, but Eloise said, 'Obviously she's a Jew,' and he turned on the water and wrapped a towel around my head. Nervously I sat down for him to comb my hair and cut it. Eloise had fixed up cheese and crackers on a plate. She went to the bathroom down the hall and at once I was conscious of his loins at my shoulder, his fingers tenderly snipping off strands of my hair. He leaned across me, brushing my breast with his hand, reaching for a cracker, and then proceeded to crunch on it near my ear.

I was a total novice where sex and seduction were concerned. My only experience was that horrible day with Honey; and then her and Ramon's relationship viewed vicariously. And so it was with a mix of horror and fascination that I felt my body respond to his body, in spite of my indifference to him, the person. I felt I was melting and only when Eloise returned could I maintain control.

He roamed around me, snipping here and there, cutting my hair to just below my ears and forming a natural bowl so it waved under, and my forehead was as clear as a nun's. He stepped back, then forward, playing with it against my cheeks until he was satisfied. The care and attention he was giving me filled me up with gratitude. Now for the mirror, he said. Come on. *It looks adorable*, cried Eloise. I followed him down the hall into the bathroom where he stood behind me, admiringly, while I looked at my new face. Not Anne Frank, I said, not Claire Bloom, or Tess of the D'Urbervilles, but it sure looks better. Thank you! Rudolph replied: My pleasure. And he placed his hands on my bottom, standing behind me, and pressed me up against the porcelain. He looked at me and I at him in the mirror, while he squeezed and kneaded me with his hands, then lifted them to my breasts and proceeded to work on them. (I remembered Honey's father with horror.) No one had touched me since that day. My knees weakened, I felt hot and nauseous and gazed into his glass face seeing an expression of grief there that only increased the gush of uncertainty throughout my limbs. Now he led me roughly out the door and into the air and up the stairs and into his room.

The only reason to mention this experience is that I discovered two things: that I was urged on by a mystifying emotion – pity. His desire had a quality of hysterical necessity about it. I now know how that works, of course, but at the time I was under the impression that I must relieve him of this necessity – cure him, be his nurse! And so I did, in this way making my first sexual experience an act of compassion. Secondly I learned that I had a body and therefore I must exist. Since he did not penetrate me but stayed outside, I was able to contemplate the reality of my own sensuality without threat.

Soon afterwards I caught glimpses of him and Eloise locking, warmly, near the stove, or the liquor cabinet, and awoke to the fact that they were lovers. How had I failed to see that before?

Months after this – I kept my hair short still – Heaven arrived back in town. He loved my new cut and so I told him on a cement block near Sather Gate about my encounter with Rudolph. Heaven flinched. I asked why and he handed me the cigarette he was smoking as if it were a peace pipe. I took a drag, and our fingers touched.

That's disgusting. I can't believe you let him near you. Don't you understand? You will hate yourself even more if you allow yourself to be somebody else's pleasure. Men are like cats. They make love to themselves against women. Ugh! I would like to erase the whole occasion of that barber. Virginity is the only way for you, Bronte. Sooner or later we will be able to get serious about our love for each other, but there is time – things to be done – between – if you know what I mean.

I don't, I do.

He eyed me kindly.

It's that horrible Honey who damaged you, raped you! Face it ... Ideally I will be your one and only.

You can be. I'll let you!

No, Sweetie, never make promises you can't keep.

I want to make a promise I can't keep. Please?

He mused on this for awhile, caressed my neck and the small of my back. I was carrying a poster protesting capital punishment and leaned on it like a crutch as he lifted me and walked me back to my place. There we crept up the back stairs without seeing Eloise or Rudolph.

And so we had our white night together. No sleep, no silence. The pigeons burbled in the eaves. I kept my hands in the sleeves of his shirt, squeezing on his muscles, and never closed my eyes for fear of missing the time and the name I was living in. When the pallor of the day lined the corners of my curtains, we both cried into a roll of paper towels. Then – within minutes – he was on his way. Before descending, he stood on the steps and handed me a pearl revolver for a toy, and gave me this advice:

It's good you are protesting injustice ... but I want you to do this for me: work with others for social change. Climb out of yourself and into the hearts of those who are poor and oppressed. Find a suitable group for your temperament and participate. Otherwise I won't be able to rest. If you have to sleep with another man, fine, but don't ever tell me about it again. Okay? I'll keep in touch, and when the time is right, we'll get serious. Till then?

I'd been turned into a she who takes orders and believes. I did most everything he said. I became part of the demonstrations and the movements in the streets around Berkeley. I screamed along with the mobs. My whole person ached for contact – i.e. love – but if I necked, I didn't get screwed. I held my nudity back and never let a hand travel further than my loins. I was bad but good, or good but bad, and like a dog's mouth, panting and watery, loping under the residential greens, all along I was restraining my appetites. I had, by him, been catapulted into a condition both mechanistic and ecstatic. I was a mongrel seeking out a gang, a manual looking for a hand.

For a good year I participated in organizing, canvassing, phoning, soliciting. I read Marx, Lenin, Mao, I watched Cuban and African liberation, I hated executions, I read Thoreau on civil disobedience, the life of Frederick Douglass, Frantz Fanon and Marguerite Duras, Doris Lessing, Julio Cortázar's *Hopscotch*. I argued with others about the usefulness of violent versus nonviolent action.

I experienced Eloise as the ultimate enemy. Sloppy and matriarchal. But I myself was to myself foreign in the fray, an ambassador from the lost. Sit-ins and thrown-from. Washed down steps by fire hoses. Out of love.

I was obsessed with the question of injustice. I wanted to witness the manifestation of a radical love that would dash the obstacles out of sight and level the authorities. A kind of love that Jesus and Buddha had prescribed and experienced. But Einstein was the true guru of our time. Music, brains, science, instinct, uncertainty, completion ... Let me through! was the cry of my days.

I was going insane from what I was seeing and feeling. I prayed to God for a sign that there would be an end to my distress. It came: A valentine from Heaven. No return address, but he sent it from Chicago: laces and ribbons on crimson silk. The sign fell from the mailman's hand, and before him, from the body of an airplane, and before that, from a bag and a man.

I prayed again: God, give me a radical love. Let me break the boundaries. God, find me a face I can believe in until Heaven returns.

Finally I was given, out of the leavings of a day, a perfect friend, a big strong freckled black-haired Irish girl with blue eyes. She was part of the Free Speech Movement but did her own work in a more extreme wing. Arrested a lot, the daughter of Catholic anarchists from New

York, she lived in a single room, had three IDs and was the first person to guess that mine was an assumed name. Sal and I did everything we could together, maintaining ourselves at a subsistence level, eating little and drinking nothing stronger than coffee. My room was bare; I used the library for my books. Sal stole hers. I only had a radio for music. She had a loving family. I had none. We often quarreled over issues and ideas, and this way strengthened and enlarged them.

I had an aversion to Utopian ideals, being a solitary, but she did not. Instead she had enormous faith in human organization and history. She was full of certitude, while I was girlish, watery, unclear. She lived through books and jumped from one to the next with the energy and excitement of an athlete. She really believed we were on the brink of social revolution, and she wanted to be in the front as a leader. We argued about the necessity to use violence, but halfheartedly, because she was at heart as non-violent as I was. She was more interested in the concept of continuing revolution and quoted Ben M'hidi in *The Battle of Algiers*: 'It's difficult to start a revolution and more difficult to sustain it and still more difficult to continue it.' She turned me on to Sartre and Camus, and through them I awoke to alienation, disgust, the spirit of revolt, and called myself an Existentialist although I still didn't know if I existed. This might explain why I never took drugs, why Sal and I never believed in 'the love revolution', why I loved Sylvia Plath and Woody Guthrie, why I went to jazz cafés and was prepared to die.

It was not more than six months into our friendship when she persuaded me to perform my first true act of civil disobedience. I would be the best person to do it, she and some guys decided, because I basically was a nobody. Since there was no record of my place in time any more, there was no one for the authorities to catch. Those early events – an uprooted infancy and second time orphaning, my new name and my invisibility – came together now as if they had been designed for this day and time. For awhile I felt more integrated a person than I ever had before. Even though I performed certain actions in the childish spirit of a dare, and often was as terrified as my targets were, for a brief time I felt my history added up and made me a perfect fraud. I never harmed a body.

I was better than anyone at keeping secrets until now.

My euphoria didn't last long before I became paranoid. Through my clandestine actions, I felt I existed too much! On the one hand I was lost to the world, and on the other hand I was leaving marks wherever I went. After about the tenth of these acts I became more reclusive and frightened than ever until I hardly ventured outside my routine at all. It didn't help that I was a girl, lectured to and bullied by everyone I worked for, from office clerk to revolutionary. Planted or stuffed into the back seats of big fat dirty cars, us girls were pitted against each other in a sisterhood of rivalry. We crouched and flirted, flaunted and concealed, we eyed each other from inside fake fur coats, mine was leopard, like the skin of a drowned movie star. Even Sal got competitive with me around the guys. Wine and cigarettes were passed around between us generously, but we were suspicious to the core of losing ground to each other. Sal was my friend from whom I only hid the secret of Heaven. I had told her about my true identity and past as an act of trust; though later I suspected she had told others. But I never mentioned the one person whose memory I threw ahead of me from one room into the next to keep me going forward. Nothing could fail if he would be there in the end, I told myself, never wondering what might happen in the middle. After all, there seemed to be no middle to my story. Just a series of beginnings and endings. Even now the whole story is something like a see-saw made of past and future.

The balance shifted again soon after I turned twenty. First the barber moved out, and then Eloise went to the hospital with liver troubles. She asked me to rent Rudolph's room, while she was gone, to anyone who seemed reliable. On a warm Saturday afternoon I was out on the steps watching the turquoise wings of a hummingbird, when Gusty arrived. Baggy pants, a white shirt, sneakers. His hair was colorless, messy. He lifted his face to look at me, his eyes a violent blue, his forehead unusually clear, straight nose, nervous mouth. An insane tennis player perhaps, or the youthful revolutionary look of a Bowery drunk. Handsome. I stepped back, at once, afraid. I knew where he would be coming from.

Is this the place where there's a room? he asked.

Yup, in there, I have the key.

I knew he must be from Boston. First we see sex, then we measure beauty, then we hear money. His nasal preppy voice, his whole demeanor, was familiar. But he looked, literally and figuratively, as if he had escaped breathless across a border. A terrified rich loner had fled the east. I let him into the room but my hands trembled.

Is this it? he asked.

Well, what's wrong? It's a nice room.

It's green.

Fifteen a week.

That's how much a month? he asked. I can't add. Uh, four times fifteen is – uh – forty-five? No wait. Four times five is twenty, add the two to the four ones and it's six. Sixty?

Slowly I nodded while he twisted his mouth around and stared at the floor.

What's your occupation? I asked him.

Student.

What of?

History. Graduate.

He assumed I was illiterate because I showed him the room. It meant I was in a servant class and was therefore inferior, but I saw him trying for a liberal approach. After all, this was California.

You know, I'm studying western culture, he said, and added: But some day I'll have to get a regular job.

But you have enough money now to cover the rent?

Sure. I guess I'll go for this room.

Eloise wants thirty dollars down.

He took it out of a sharp brown leather wallet stuffed, I could see, with cash, and glared at me.

What's your name? he asked.

Bronte Wilde.

God, that could only happen in California.

Really? What's yours?

Augustus – well, Gusty – Winter.

I reserved my remarks. He held out his hand, and I shook it.

When are you moving in?

Now! My stuff is in the car out front.

I'll help you then.

So we went down together. He had Massachusetts license plates all right and I remembered a girl who went to the Mystic School with me – Lizzy Winter – who had colorless curly hair and blue eyes like his. She used to stare longingly at our little gang of outcasts: Henny, Libby, Honey and me. I didn't open my mouth. We carried things up, one load after another. He was shy but charming. Polite, solicitous, humorous and above all, for me, familiar. He was nostalgia, I climbed in. He was home, I ran along clinging after him. I might have sniffed danger but I was reckless. His charm was familiar to me and heartbreaking; he was either self-deprecating or self-adoring because he was always self-referential. He was privileged, feminine. Attention was focused on him because of the energy of his own responses to himself. I think this is the essence of what they call a magnetic personality (or narcissism). In any case, I was a sucker for his smiles, his jokes, his sallies into neurosis, even as I tried to sustain a serious quarrel with him. The quarrel was political, invariably. His snobbery and conservatism were accompanied by facts, facts, facts. He knew the news of the week as well as he knew the news of the centuries. Who was related to whom, what their property was, which war destroyed what clan, etc. Whenever I expressed a strong opinion, he shot it down with a series of facts. His cynicism was profound and spreading faster underground than any leftist ideology. Reason is the subtlest oppressor there is and its arsenal is cynicism.

Our argument was ancient: rich against poor, have against have-not, willpower against destiny. He was on the side of the haves, he was one of them, and he believed in individualism in a nineteenth century kind of way. He was for free enterprise, for the survival of the fittest. Yes, it was Social Darwinism in the twentieth century. I could have and be anything I wanted, he insisted, then joked that 'class' was not something that I could ever acquire. If I wanted to be rich, I could be rich in the grand old spirit of the robber barons; there was nothing to stop me. And if I didn't want to be rich, then I had no right to hate those who did. My anger he figured was a form of envy.

It's not anger. It's revulsion, I whispered.

He was persuasive with his smiles, his gestures, and his depreciation of his own value. I began to flounder. I began to believe in democracy rather than socialism, I began to revise my feelings about class and economics. It is awful to write it down, and in such simplistic terms, but the process, as I see it now, was inevitable. Not long after his arrival, I constantly dreamt of Alice and Henry. They were always taking me somewhere encased in the comforts of home – chandeliers, soft rugs, pianos, food. These goods were the material manifestations of the good they wished for me, the love they had for me. They beckoned me back to soft gold cones and protection. I stretched to follow, but was invariably checked by nudity, missed train connections, wrong directions and stunning sadness.

After one of these nightmares, I woke up at dawn and went out on my wooden balcony. Down the dewy steps, pale in the light, clutching my body in my pajamas and not liking the feel of it. For no matter how little I ate and weighed, I still had large breasts, 'a good if starved pro-letarian build,' as Sal liked to call it. Gusty came to his door and looked out.

Oh, he said. I thought it was a stranger.

Maybe it is, I said.

He hung out the door, in t-shirt and shorts, gristly and mean-looking. I gave him a contemptuous look, for I was trying to deal with the terror of my dreams as best I could.

You woke me up, he said.

I have to go to work in a few minutes.

Well, what are you doing now? he asked.

Enjoying the birds, I love them.

He didn't care and shut the door. I went on down, feeling hurt and depressed by dreams of home. The grass was too cold, too wet, it was unpleasant, but a few birds began their warble and I listened to them calling back and forth a score of messages and I thought of my piano with embarrassment. How could I have let all of it go so casually? 'When angels or spirits speak with man, they speak in his own language, from his memory,' Swedenborg wrote. It was as if a spirit had flown around my sleeping head and let in a whole gush of sounds.

Gusty did more than just remind me of my childhood, my home. He was my home. Wine from Algeria could be sipped as if it were the blood of Camus. Breath from Boston could be breathed like the breezes over the Charles River. When I was near Gusty, I didn't need to stifle a yearning for the familiar; I needed to stifle my dread of it. I was now attracted to a person who represented the world I had casually rejected. The attraction increased the paranoia which had already become the metaphor for my whole condition. The ineffectuality of my life as a body without a name had a nearly suicidal set of reverberations. I breathed hard on the bus to work, I swooned. I was sure the police were after me, only one step behind the CIA; and at the same time, I was equally sure nobody knew I existed at all. It was only the figure of Gusty who came to reassure me that I had a history. Some reassurance. He was both messenger and enemy.

Now I began to feel that time might not be a seemingly immobile space through which our bodies moved, checking off our progress by the objects we left behind. Instead time felt like an actual place, a tidepool, say, where a person whirled around and around, encountering the same people again and again, and where there was no chance of escape. I longed for someone to talk to, but sadly Heaven was the only one to whom I could speak about these thoughts, knowing I would be understood. And he was too far and long gone then to help me. So I called Sal.

Obediently she arrived, bearing food. She thought I wanted to return to active duty, running around San Francisco stirring up trouble. I said no. We had a quarrel about the necessity for non-violent terrorism versus conventional political action. The quarrel helped me elucidate the terror I was feeling in my psyche. By objectifying the story of outrage, I could see what was happening to me internally.

What is this? she wondered aloud. How can you possibly believe that your ordinary congressman is going to do anything about changing the status quo? How can you believe in ballots and votes after all that's happened in the name of democracy? We're all being fed lies. From Chicago to Vietnam is a trail of democratic paperwork. And you defend it? What's got into you? Are you falling back on the middle class attitudes of your parents? You must be scared shitless, you look famished, you must be having a breakdown.

I felt as if I was unpacking my words on the roof of my mouth, it was so hard to utter a sentence, to believe in the common sense of the vocabulary, the grammar.

Please, I don't, come on, I mean, it's just, you don't mean, try, the reason, well, a guess, I feel, it's awful, but really, I want, I guess, to be – well, safe.

Safe? You want to be safe? So do I, so do the Vietnamese, so do all the fucked-over people in Africa, Latin America, and the South. Make the world safe for democracy? Is that what you're talking about? Have we made the world safe for others or has the US of A been on a rampage of destruction and greed? Like Rome. Yes, like Rome! Read your history books again, kid, and remember your roots in a Europe that is rotten to the core. Did Germany make itself safe in the 30s? Safety is a fucking luxury at this date in time. If we don't watch out and be willing to make sacrifices, it will be the end of fucking civilization, democracy included. It's a one-way street, you can't turn back, not once you've really seen what a hypocrisy it all is.

Democracy rhymes with hypocrisy for a good reason. And don't tell me you agree but America is still the best country to live in, because how do you know if that's true? How do you know if good values don't compensate for a clean bathroom? How do you know if it wouldn't be a deeper and more humane existence if you lived in a hutch with people who loved each other and shared everything? Safe. Nobody is safe as long as one person is being fucked-over. Nobody is safe as long as there is suffering in the world, unjustly afflicted. We all can agree that life is unfair, right? It is. From day one. But don't let day two, three, four, compound the original imbalance. The point is to make people fulfill their potential, all people, and not to take advantage of the original injustice and use it to get ahead, get power. The thing is, kid, the world isn't safe. And until people really get it, and understand that this bourgeois notion of safety is a hype, then we will go on believing in the righteousness of a democracy which is really raping and mutilating other people. Safe! I can't believe you, of all people, said that!

Sorry, but ...

My breath was short, I was dizzy and hot and experienced sound as a smashing of brass on glass. I heard, but withdrew from the message. I put a pillow over my ears and shut my eyes. Sal pulled it off and dragged me out on the balcony. The air was warm and smelled sweetly of night-blooming jasmine. She unwrapped lox, cream cheese, bagels, coffee. These maternal acts were reassuring, as was her rough treatment of me. I leaned against her, beginning to breathe (believe) again. She fed me. She talked. I pushed the glasses up her nose when they slid down.

You okay? she asked through teeth filled with cheese.

No, fine, no, yes, fine, I'm.

Listen. I don't want to force you to get into action again.

If I could, just, I mean, well, *travel!* I screamed.

Travel? You can.

Where, when, how?

We'll figure it out. Sorry, Bronte, I just remembered what a fucked-up childhood you had, sorry, I forgot who I was talking to. You of all people should know.

Now we heard crunching on the path at the side of the house, footsteps, and we stopped talking. Gusty was coming up the steps. He was oblivious to our presence at first. Then, at his door, he looked up and saw us.

Hi there, he called.

Hi, I said thumping inside, come on up.

He lifted up a paper bag shaped like a sawed-off shotgun. Want some wine? I said yes and he got his corkscrew and I got cups. It was an expensive kind of French wine, and a new experience for me. Sal looked at her watch and refused to drink. She stared at the moonlight on the branches and eyed Gusty, who squatted beside me.

Green is supposed to be a soothing color, said Gusty.

Maybe that's why the leaves are green, said Sal.

Or that's why green is soothing. In any case, I used to be in this place – a hospital – I was, well, I cracked up once – for months actually – and the room was pale green. And now the room downstairs is green, too, and it makes me very uneasy.

But you said it's soothing, said Sal.

It isn't when the association is wrong, apparently.

Does the grass bother you? asked Sal. I could see she thought Gusty was a creep.

Why don't you move? asked Sal.

In general, I like this place.

You must've had a hard life, if you have to worry about the color scheme of your room.

Well, it is important, I said.

Oh yeah?

I'm sorry, said Gusty, I didn't mean to start anything or interrupt.

He got up and Sal nodded vigorously.

I'll help you paint your room, I told him.

Now that's a good idea.

Oh my God, Sal groaned and put on her leathers. Gusty looked around the trees. His glazed and abstract face reminded me of someone, made him all the more familiar. Maybe it was Henry? or Honey? It caused me pain. He drifted down the stairs with his bottle in his hand, and I felt sorry for him. As if I knew his past and future in advance, I pitied and forgave him in a swoop.

I didn't know he had been sick, I said quickly.

Had been? He is!

Well, he's just eccentric.

Over-bred is the word.

Maybe.

You like him, don't you?

What do you mean, you make it sound like a dirty word.

It is, in this case, said Sal. I can smell a Republican.

She was seeing through me. She got up to go to her Harley, uneasy with what she had witnessed, and launched into plans for our assault on the latest HUAC meetings in San Francisco, telling me how she would enter the courtroom separate from her friends, and only heckle after others had.

The FBI will know you're there even before you get there, I said.

So what? Want to come along?

No. If I, well, you know, get picked up, it's, oh well. Sal stared away from me as if I was vomiting. You need to get normal, she said. Go see my mother. Have some soup.

Soup?

Minestrone.

Minister to me.

I would but you don't want it from me, she said.

No, well, don't – I do.

My mother always told me the world is divided into three categories: socialists, capitalists and artists. Know what an artist is? Well, I'd rather see you with one of them than with a capitalist. Any day.

She drifted down the steps then and into a well of leafy shadows.

Often being with Gusty was like entering a hospital; an oppressive and sickly atmosphere surrounded his body, and an array of danger signals. I felt I might catch every thought and emotion that coursed through his bloodstream. Yet I was paralyzed, immunized, couldn't leave! This paralysis proved to me how far I had strayed. I was now more lost than free. While my criminal acts plagued me, and suffused my days with paranoia, I was simultaneously convinced I didn't exist now and never really had.

I had to quit my job. I could no longer believe I was not under surveillance. The typewriter keys and files grew meaningless and therefore dangerous under my newly-acquired illness. I had spent little, fortunately, and I began to live off my savings, now altering my needs to keep up with his. Wine, whiskey, pills to recover. I don't like to write this down, though many years have passed since then, because the memory still affects me as much as the experience did.

First we painted his room white. He often asked me about Sal and the guys, what my relationship was with them, where did I meet them, where was she from, was she politically subversive, a lesbian? He pummeled me with questions about my life too, delving in a way I had not encountered before. It was serious cross-examination. It was the sort of questioning that is motivated by a desire for some evil to be revealed. I lied all the way down the line and in my gratitude for his interest, I gave little dollops of truth only when it didn't involve facts. I believed that he, unlike the imminent enemy coming to get me, asked these questions in a spirit of love for me, and I convinced myself that the information he was seeking was only a story that would make him jealous. Right off I had to lie, when he asked me the inevitable and normal questions.

So where do you come from? Who are your parents?

Now my usual story failed me here. If I told him he would ask other questions that I could not answer. He would ask for the names of mental hospitals and symphony orchestras. I would be all washed up.

I just have a mother. She's a waitress in Sonoma, I said.

He glared at me. His face and hair were speckled with white paint.

A waitress. How come you are so well read?

Jesus, you're a snob, I said.

I know I am.

Don't you hate yourself?

Yes, but not because I'm a snob.

We stepped outside for fresh air. The paint fumes were nauseating.

Why can't I read Proust and work as an account-
ant? Why can't I play Mozart and go to public schools?
You must be very innocent, if you think the world is
divided so carefully into two parts.

He smiled amiably.

You'll have to teach me some things, he said.

It was pathetic how much I wanted to say: 'My name is
Mary Casement and maybe we know some of the same
people.' On the other hand, I feared that revelation more
than anything. He didn't want me to be Mary Casement
at all, he wanted me to be the daughter of a waitress
from Sonoma. I was being eaten alive by my own lies.

What followed, followed fast. Eloise gave us drinks to
reward us for painting the room. Then she cooked up
some macaroni and cheese and we sat around her
kitchen getting smashed. A goddess must have been
watching out for me, for at one point Gusty said,

Imagine Bronte as the daughter of a waitress.

What for? asked Eloise.

And she gave me a look demanding an explanation.
Instinct told her to be on guard, to stand before me protectively. I just stared back, my lips curling behind my
hand.

I just can't see her coming from that kind of back-
ground, he said with a misty smile at me. Eloise
shrugged.

That's why she's such a great little cook, said
Eloise. You should taste her Eggs Benedict.

(Now the whole scene could have been reversed with disastrous consequences for me. Eloise could have started it, by saying, Imagine Bronte as the daughter of a nutty violinist! The game, then, would be up. I smiled at her, and she at me. I would have to explain later.)

The alcohol in each person had saved me. I got very drunk and I remember hearing the two of them discussing the Civil Rights Movement as if it were an adolescent rebellion. They caught my expression of outrage and laughed, calling me 'parlor pink'. I left them and roamed the house ripping at my hair and face, wanting to put wounds into their condescension. My mouth was dry and sealed like the sticky parchment of a collaborator.

I remembered Sal saying, 'Any thinking person who's not a revolutionary is a fucking wimp.' And, too: 'The whole point of non-violent terrorism is to instill fear in the enemy. Make him uneasy. Make him fear the thief in the night every night. Wait till he's fat and full and dozing. Get him off guard. Every time.'

I went down to the kitchen and took a piece of steak out of the freezer, carried it upstairs and laid it on Eloise's pillow. Then, weaving unsteadily down the stairs, I called a pleasant goodnight to them. Gusty came out to follow me. And at the door of his room he said he couldn't sleep in there because of the smell of paint. Can I sleep with you? he asked.

On the floor, I told him coldly.

Obediently he fell into a sleeping bag beside my bed and snored loudly, sprouting halfway out of the bag, his cheek on the floor. We both slept hard, and when we woke up it was Monday, and I was late for work.

Don't go, he said. Call in and say you're sick.

Which I was; and I did call in sick and thus began my withdrawal from the pattern of my life. I didn't go to work or meetings, I didn't read the papers, I didn't read *The Rebel* by Camus as I had been planning to do. I read little. I bought a guitar instead and sat in my room teaching myself songs. I smoked up a storm and waited for Gusty to come home from his classes. It was like riding a dragon. I wanted to woo and impress him, to make him faint at my knees and suffer with love; then I would poison him, or something to that effect. Say I was madly in love with him, the symptoms were the same, but I can't exactly say it was love myself.

We slept together after an odd scene one night. He started crying into his beer, literally, and I didn't know what to do. Contrary to myth, the sight of another in tears does not always produce a sympathetic effect in the witness. I didn't know what was happening. I watched him in the way the moon watched me. I stared until he had gained his self-control and rubbed the tears from his cheeks.

I'm sorry, he said.

What for?

I'm not being fair to you.

In what way?

It's a long story.

I love long stories, tell me.

His eyes, red-rimmed and bright blue, burned. He was a smooth-skinned and rumpled boy, handsome to me always, and now. He produced, at odd moments, a rush of maternal pity, hot milk, in my veins.

I always thought I would learn, he said. No – get something from other people. I mean, I thought everyone knew something I didn't know and if I stuck with them, I'd acquire that secret wisdom and be saved. Do you know what I mean?

I pretended I did and nodded.

Well, you, see, seem to have a strength and self-sufficiency buried in you. And I want it to rub off on me. But, you know, you're not what one would call a raving beauty, according to my type, although you're growing on me; and I'm a sucker when it comes to knock-out beauty. I like to walk down the street with a pretty girl beside me. I've never been with a girl who wasn't outstanding before. But I've never been away from a certain environment before either. Here it doesn't seem to matter so much. I mean, people seem more relaxed, and I guess I don't have anyone around I especially want to impress. Do you know what I mean?

Unfortunately I did.

Well, it's obviously important for my development that I learn how to love someone for their character, and not for their face. It sounds so obvious, but really it isn't.

He moved over beside my bed and sat at my feet. He took my hand and held it to his lips.

Will you let me try to learn how to love you?

It's a long sentence, but I'll try, I said.

He stood up and pulled me against him.

Let's fuck, he said, trying to sound debonair.

The words did not fit his character, and I laughed. He was trembling as if I were a lawyer and he was in court. I asked him to repeat that statement, please, but he couldn't, he was mute. I told him he could lie beside me but that was all, and the color returned to his cheeks, his shoulders eased.

You a virgin or something? he asked.

I love someone already, I told him.

He didn't care who, or ask a single question about this revelation. He just smoothed down the hairs on his arms, and slipped into the sheets beside me, and didn't touch me.

Mercy is a cruel word; you have to beg for it. Justice is quite different, an achievement to be pursued. When I asked the universe for mercy, then, I knew I was a slave to love. The next day I waited for Gusty to return from his classes, I feared his mood. The sexless night before might make him leave me. I was like Honey, sick for love. I tore my brush through my hair believing I would die if he left or was mad at me. Was this love?

But he surprised me by returning early in a happy state of mind. He came right to me and planted a kiss between my brows. In his bag he carried a bottle of wine, some Monterey Jack, and a loaf of bread. He put them out on the sunlit table and we sat down to eat. He told me about his classes and I listened quietly, if not sullenly. I didn't want him to know how good I felt, for fear it would ruin everything. Instinct warned me that the worst I could do was to show pleasure. Indifference and a constant expression of dissatisfaction would keep him near. Should I move to embrace him, he would withdraw; he would be the sullen one. So I looked bored. His eyes, capsules of blue sky, flew around uneasily.

Tell me that long story, now, I told him.

Why now?

I want to know where you come from.

There is no happier topic of conversation for a man than himself, according to Heaven. Gusty lounged on my bed with a glass of wine in a position reminiscent of famous French courtesans.

HIS STORY

I was born in Brookline, Massachusetts, the only son of a bitch and a bastard. My father is my namesake. He is his father's namesake. They started out in England as blacksmiths and thieves. And we ended up in New England rich. My mother is a rough diamond. A biddy and thin. You see them everywhere. Rockefeller women. Pat Nixon. Whittled down by rain, sun, nerves and men to totem poles, masks. Empty shrines.

I sometimes occupied a large bedroom down the hall from theirs, but not often. For I was sent away to school. We had maids and cooks. I have one sister who is two years older than me and a Catholic convert. My parents went to church regularly, Episcopalian, to ask for more good luck. Superstitious, atheists. I went to prep schools where I was captain of the hockey team and a writer. I wrote stories and poems. I was a god. Everyone adored and obeyed me. I had a secret passion for myself which only increased my charms for others. It was clear I needed no one. Girls at other schools who came to our dances on weekends went home and wrote love poems about me. I was referred to as Apollo or Brookline's answer to James Dean. They loved me for being so mean.

Next stage was Brandeis which I chose as an antidote to the Ivy League circuit. I was, you see, beginning to weaken under the pressures of my own status. Being a god isn't easy. I was sick of myself, my onanistic, solipsistic life. (Do you know what those words mean? Probably not, thank God.) But I was scared of girls who, because of their sex, embodied my mother's rigid and castrating attitudes. At last I cracked up and was sent off to an expensive mental hospital for awhile.

When I returned to college in a year I was able to date pretty girls and study for high grades, but it was all phony. After graduation, I cracked up again and was sent to another expensive mental hospital in western Massachusetts where I stayed for six months. (This was only one year ago.) I met a girl there and, in the process of reviving her from a long sleep, I rehabilitated myself, got interested in psychology, and came to California, where I met you.

Yeah, but what about that girl?

What I did to this girl is not very nice. She was a writer – not published or anything – but she had this pile of diaries and poems hidden away – love poems mostly, things about her first love kind of thing. Anyway, she went through this big production about showing them to me. I was the first person who had ever read them. She said even her analyst wouldn't be able to appreciate their meaning, so I mustn't laugh at her. I read them, seriously, and they were very good. That was the shock, they were good. But I hated them. They were competition. I wanted to own her. So I burned all of them one day. That way, see, I would be the only one, ever, who would have read them. And when it was over, when she found out, she went berserk, apparently it was the second time, she tried to kill me, that was a first, but they say it was good for her, the trauma of loss, because she got a lot of shit out of her system. Soon after I left. And I hear she's okay now. Sort of.

You still own her.

I know.

What's her name?

I won't tell you.

Why not?

Then her presence would come between us.

All this was spoken in his classy, nasal, bemused voice. The tone, even more than the words, drew me back. I was rowing against the tide which was carrying me home. I watched him as he lay there, smoking, and the terrible thing he did to the nameless female seemed welded to his flesh. I wouldn't forget it or forgive it. If only I could sit in judgment over him forever like this. But my own dishonest position put a blight on my abilities to condemn. At least he told the truth. He waved me over, but I don't like to be waved over.

What, I said.

Come here.

What for?

You know what for.

You come here, I said. He stared at me.

Sometimes you sound like you come from Boston, he said.

Oh, how?

Your accent.

I tend to pick up accents. It must be yours.

All right. Come here.

I relented, slipping over to the bed with a scowl. He pulled me down. The sun shone on his shoes. He lay over me like a cadaver – gone cold, inert. Yet the worm stirred, lifted, and pressed against my thigh. My face stayed turned aside, my eyes opened wide, as he put it to me blindly. My arms were wrapped around his narrow frame, and my gaze was steady, staring at the window until my eyes burned, and I allowed the simulation of love to work on my memory. Then I believed I was back with Heaven again. And in my imagination I strained to see him. Like the one peach you don't need to press to test its ripeness, a golden brown hue emanated from Heaven. There would be no touching, yet how he touched me! My eyes burned and drew tears. I was with the wrong man!

I closed my eyes and as in so many dreams there was – way behind the vision of Heaven – a miniature panorama with a touch of shade across it, a vista as if painted in water. I saw pale upright stones, snow, and mountains – no animals, but I knew they were around. It was a place I seemed to remember, if only because I saw it with my eyes closed. It was perhaps the landscape of my own brain, or a landscape already imprinted in my own brain. I gazed at the distant wash and saw letters fall from the sky – an N, a B, an O – and they were white and sharp, like spears of ice.

I called to Heaven, and now two hummingbirds, turquoise, luminous, settled in front of my eyes. I called again to Heaven to come back, but instead the birds turned into two long-gowned flying little women, angels who played like marionettes in the air. Heaven's warmth had been replaced by air, by cold, by objectivity, by Gusty.

One afternoon I joined Eloise in her garden full of nut trees and squashed-up plants. She did not have a green thumb. All the shrubs and flowerbeds looked as if an elephant had recently thundered through. We sat on tattered aluminum chairs and drank mint juleps. (She had once mentioned the meat on her pillow, roaring with laughter at having been so drunk that she threw steak on the bed instead of the stove!) Gusty was at school or the library. I was, by then, a worse wreck of nerves than ever, vertiginous seizures overcame me in stores and on the streets, my phobias multiplied. I felt as if I had caught them from Gusty like a flu. His fears seemed to seep into my skin from his sweat, his breath. How could I escape it now? Since he had begun to make love to me, I tasted his mouth in mine, and smelled his skin in passing breezes.

'What's eating you?' asked Eloise.

I looked away.

Come on, Miss Prudence. You're in love? Is that so bad? Something's eating you.

She faced the sun with shut eyes. I stared at her profile, her reddish eyelashes flickering, her full painted lips pressed tight.

You know, you're my little girl. I always wanted a little girl and you fit the bill. I don't know why you're telling that boy your mother is a waitress, because she isn't but I wish you'd tell big Mama here, so I could help you out.'

The ice in my glass rattled. I drew a deep breath, then in a slow whizz of air let it all out. The facts of my life deflated me. I told her my real name was Mary Casement and I came from Boston. I had no family because of what happened first during the war and then later in Massachusetts and now I wanted to keep it that way. It was my fate to be uprooted. She didn't even shift the skin on her face, but seemed nearly asleep listening.

Don't tell Gusty, I begged her, please!

You haven't told me very much, she said.

There isn't much to tell.

Okay, okay, but I think you're running away. And why don't you tell Gusty? It isn't fair to him, really, to keep him in the dark. What if he wants to marry you one of these days? Then you'll really be in hot water, no birth certificate.

Believe me, that won't happen, I said and explained what a snob he was. I come from gypsies, remember.

Then what are you doing with him? I don't understand you, my friend, and I'm a little peeved to boot. For four-odd years now you've been leading me to believe you were something that you're not. You're probably some kind of radical Jewish type and I've been wasting all my emotions worrying about your situation. You can't just go around doing this to people. I won't feel sorry for you again.

She gave me a sidelong glance, then clamped shut on the sun again. My lips quivered, tears rolled.

If I hadn't told you, I said, everything would be all right.

She thought about this for awhile, then she said,

Please tell that boy the truth. Before it goes too far. I don't want any trouble under my roof, you understand?

I told her I did although I didn't and went inside. I was not amused, as Heaven would say. I had made a profound tactical error; the game was up. Shortly thereafter I was hiding (there's no other word for it) in my room when Sal came pounding on the door.

Where've you been? she demanded.

Here.

Well, there's a lot going on. We need you.

I was curled into my chair in a sweat. I wanted her to go. It was the one longing in my mind. She looked around the room with a rather brutal tactless eye.

Seeing that guy downstairs? she asked.

Yup.

I thought so. The little prick. Reeks of privilege. You look awful. Why don't you go down south, get into action again? It would do you good.

I rubbed my face and eyes hard.

I'll call you, I told her.

No you won't. I'm going away soon myself.

Where?

New York first, then Mississippi. Why don't you come back with me? No strings attached. I could use the company on the drive, and you could stay with my people. My mother will mother you. You need to get away from these CIA jocks. They're destroyers.

I looked at her with a feeling of joy because she seemed to understand how badly I felt and not to judge me. She gave me her parents' address in New York and a sudden uncharacteristic embrace, then left at full speed, enviable in her energy, her equivalent hope.

(God, find me a savior! A nun, a nurse, anyone ... Here I am and I pray to industrial waste heaps out in the steam of meadows and see the birds rise from my mouth. The point is this: we are turned inside out. Or – how to put it – the way our portions of consciousness receive their content is by turning the senses right around, so what we first receive and then perceive is the interior of our own bodies. Not the world at all. Did someone else already think of this? I'm anxious because of my gender always being nice. I don't want to steal anyone's ideas though I've noticed many things. If I see a way to solve a problem and tell my boyfriend about it, he always, always argues and says why it has to be the way he has inherited or arranged it. But within a matter of weeks he has done what I suggested but never once said: 'You were right, thank you, I should have listened.' No gratitude, no acknowledgement. He doesn't love me. So what he does is called appropriation and what I do is called reiteration.)

Gusty told me I was a paranoid schizophrenic. He told

me I should see an analyst. If my tongue slipped on a word, I had revealed myself. I asked him what he was.

An aristocrat, he said. Ha!

I don't mean that.

I cried. He laughed. I cried. He laughed. I saw him and Eloise as dangerous. My doubts confirmed (in my mind) his accusations on my mental health. He was gentle as a therapist and as evasive, but his imagination was the most cruel I had ever encountered. I had no arms to fight with on that level, in that way. I was drawn, instead, to his way of thinking as a fly is drawn to honey or as honey is drawn by bees to the hive or as honey is hung in the trees by bees who will sting; he hung like honey on my heavy paws. He was glued to my body, sweet, where he finally told me the girlfriend's name, the sick one, the poet, the burnt-out blonde, the one he tried to avoid naming but, finally, one night in darkness, after my probing, did: HONEY FIGGIS.

Call it a literary coincidence or call it providence; say I planned it, but in any case you will be ignoring a whole range of historical events which are stranger than fiction. Just read the annals of occult happenings, witness how war imitates nature, be on guard all the time for the witchcraft in your own perceptions, and you will know that this was both true and unfathomable. Over me grew such blinding horror, I gave in and didn't struggle anymore. I had run in a circle.

When I heard her name I felt my whole system of perception shift to a new level. I might as well have been on a slow-acting acid. I began to approach each day with the stealth of a detective, I saw patterns where before I had seen accidents. Leaves fell in time to my music. People turned corners in pace with my thoughts. Just as O on the phone is for Operator, everything fit on a clever scale. I talked to myself and to God who was a better You than you had ever been. Most of the time, I stayed in my room and waited for the next part of the plot to unfold.

When it unfolded, I was not surprised, but welcoming. Eloise told Gusty my true story which proved what I had suspected but ignored – that the enemy always reveals itself sooner or later because it has to publicize and justify its own cynicism. You may be able to live and work with someone you are opposed to for a long time, but in the end you are forced to engage in battle. Eloise wanted to see some action, I guess. She really was every man's ally. So in came Gusty one evening, around nine, and from his smile I guessed what had happened. I curled in a ball under my blankets and waited.

Mary Casement, he said.

I was an invisible lump, a baby in a pregnant belly, where he stood over me. I thought of my mum who carried me in her slime, fed me with her blood, let my wastes flow out of her legs, transported me through rooms full of voices and music I would never identify, honking horns, her own laughter or shouts. Ripped away like a button off her coat. Who was she, and where?

He stroked the lump with his hand, then shoved me over with his bottom, sitting down. I was smothering under those covers, but rolled in tighter praying for a revelation of God and meaning. He laughed excitedly and pulled back the blankets. Soft light came over me.

Don't be ashamed, he said.

I'm not, I'm not.

He told me exactly what I had told Eloise. He was dying for more, but it wasn't like Heaven asking for more. This was the rape of the media, his longing to interpret my story, to pour his ideas all over my words, photographs snapping in his head, objective, analytical to the end.

Fine, please go away, I told him.

Don't be like that. I'm your friend, trust me.

I've got to think. Get out.

But he wouldn't leave. The longer he stayed, the less I wanted a mother or a lover or annihilation. I just wanted to be alone and running. To take a plane or a bus or a train alone, alone. Riddled with phobias by now, complete isolation and anonymity was my idea of happiness.

Don't you have any family left? he asked.

No.

Any friends?

Just one.

So you should go back east and see him, Gusty advised.

East? I don't know where he is.

You must have one girlfriend.

Well, then, yes.

Who? Why not her? he asked.

You'll see. Look in that little drawer. A photograph of her.

He opened the drawer in my bedside table, where I had a little packet of precious things: a postcard and the valentine from Heaven, and the photograph of Honey I had carried in my wallet for years. He scrutinized the picture, his cheeks burned, he held it closer to the light.

What's her name?

You know.

Incredible, he croaked and took a kind of seizure, grasping his abdomen and rolling around. I didn't know if he was laughing or crying, but I snatched the picture away before he could injure it. My last card, played.

This is the women's penitentiary. This is the State Hospital for crazies. This is the house of an exile. This is the back room of the worst job of the year in the State Unemployment Office. This is the WACS barracks. This is the inspection on the Canadian border. This is the hat-stitchers' factory. The topless nightclub dressing room. The kitchen, the bedroom, the bathroom, the dressing room in the biggest department store in the biggest shopping mall in the world. This is the light-house. This is the place where all the guns are stored, the hideout, the hole crawling with the people you fear. This is the human body at work. This is the human body at work in a place made and run by other human bodies. This is the human body at work in a place made and run by other human bodies who were made by human bodies who live in a tent bent by gravity and nothing else.

A pause: to dig at the narrative from within. A contradiction is not a paradox, but there is a connection. I am now convinced that action is everything. Yet you can't act if you can't act. You can't be twenty if you are fifteen. You can't be good if you are bad. You can't be easy if you are tense. You can't be kind if you are mean. You can't be revolutionary if you are bourgeois. You can't be a man if you are a woman. You can't be pale if you are dark. You can't be tall if you are small. You can't be a mother if you are barren. You can't be a singer if you have no voice. You can't be loving if you hate someone. You can't be forgiving if you seek revenge. You can't be sane if you are deranged. You can't be angry if you are content. You can't be asleep if you are awake. You can't be truthful if you tell lies. And all these facts have to be faced sooner or later, and more, too.

I'm just as scared as you are of the giant asleep in the woods, with his shoes off, snoring. How the light dapples his immense body. How the streams part at his head and pass down his sides and along his enormous legs. Every part of him is giant, because he is a giant. His pants, his shoes, his socks, his jacket, his Adam's apple, his penis, his bellybutton, his teeth. I'm just as scared as you are of what will happen when he wakes up and rises above the trees, and lifts up his legs, his shadow covering my cottage roof. He will stretch his arm and roar. He is a giant and everything he does springs from the immense facts of his existence. There is nothing he can do that will surprise us. We already know that a giant does giant things. What follows is inevitable. It will be what happens when a giant moves. It will be what happens when a building falls. It will be what happens when a piece of glass falls out of a window and pierces the roof of your head. It will be what happens when the big quake hits California, or what happens when your children are sucked down a whirlpool and you never see them again. The sky will shake down a blanket, the sun will disappear. You will try to grasp hold of the giant's shoe, but, for some incredible reason, it won't work, it actually won't work and you will be hurled into the eye of darkness, amazed at your weakness. The important thing, then, is to let that giant sleep. Don't make a sound. Don't act up. Sneak around. You will live in a state of perpetual dread, you will never exceed your own expectations, for fear this transgression will release havoc. At least you will keep the peace. I am telling you this so you won't mistake my acceptance of closure for righteousness.

Nothing comes free of charge. Each individual trait has its price. If I am generous, I am extravagant. If I am careful, I am also stingy. If I am forgiving, I am also self-denigrating. If I am kind, I am also demanding. If I am curious, I am also reckless. If I am starving, I will rob to eat. If I am faithful, I am also dependent. If I am passionate, I am also jealous. If I love, I am driven mad with fear for the one I love. If I hate, I am driven mad resisting my violence. So I try to play it all down. The perfect person lives alone.

Honey is standing before me, dripping gold. We are having French toast and coffee at a restaurant in a big slot paradise beside Lake Tahoe. The turquoise circle of water rimmed by pine and an ice blue sky are visible through a plate glass window. Two people are playing the slots nearby, but the place is basically empty. Dawn. An emporium of ghosts, gleaming wax-yellow floors. Cars drift by outside, flashing so I have to turn away, too bright. Maple syrup drips down Honey's chin, she wipes it away with a napkin and smiles all sweetness, at me. She speaks.

After I eat, I always smell of what I eat. Or that's what Gusty says. Babies do that, too. When Lotus was nine months, every morning she had oatmeal in molasses – the iron was good for her – in molasses, black strap, you know – and all day she smelled of it. I would put my face in her neck and take a deep drag of her fragrant skin. Babies, I love them. Nursing especially. It's the reward, for me, of horrible pregnancy. Those lips clamping and sucking – well, it's better than any orgasm, it feels like the baby is actually sucking an emotion out of me and makes me think that our chemicals and our emotions are the same thing, and you can extract happiness, say, if you know how and carry it around in a little beaker for any-one who needs it to take a sip. Now I know some people just don't get that much of a kick out of breast-feeding – like you, probably – some people think I'm crazy to have so many children. But I can't explain it, I mean I want to kill them sometimes, but every time I have one I feel I have performed a miracle or participated in an act of divine intervention, it gives me a sense of my importance, you know, it's hard to explain, but I love the crucifixion of childbirth, the red-black agony that precedes the squirm of release. And I'm not very sexual, I don't really like sex, not with someone anyway, I didn't even like it with Ramon. Big deal, get it over with. For me the point of it is having a baby nine months later. Luckily Gusty isn't a great lover either, as you know, he doesn't care much one way or the other, so we just get pregnant every time we do it. I never believe all those statistical women who say they have sex two times a week, they're lying, that's why they're statistics, they're myths. But anyway Gusty is really a wonderful father, devoted, and we are really proud of our brood, we dote on every one of them, and I'm sure they are so great because they feel this love all the time. You'll just have to come to our home some day and meet them. And brings yours too, of course.

Now Gusty appears from the men's room with his newspaper, and his hair is prematurely gray. He caresses her shoulders from behind, her yellow dress which clings like nylon to her two tiny breasts, and says it's time for them to go. My panic is concealed behind my dark glasses, I pick my purse up from the floor, the first to rise. They have a plane to catch. They will drive down the mountains, east, in a rented red Buick Riviera, and I will drive up into the mountains, west, in my blue Citroen. We will all kiss cheeks goodbye. I will show nothing of my emotions even when alone on the road.

I have a little fig tree. Nothing will it bear. It curls outside my house. It always reminds me of something. I have a row of lettuce, poorly planted, too close together, crinkly brown at the edges. My house is built in a peculiar chalet style, fitting for mountain life. So far spring flooding has not eroded its foundation. Nonetheless I wonder how long we will last here. We have no close neighbors. A long asphalt driveway winds down to the highway, where the kids wait for their school bus. Hoods, green, all year round, evergreen, redwood. The maroon smell of needle padding under foot. Sometimes sinister. But flakes of snow drifting from a yellow sky are a kind of relief, here, sugaring these monastic trees. We have been waiting for it all year. Inside the house there is no silence ever. Small rooms junked with toys, a round table junked with papers and silverware. A piano whose keys have been crayoned on. On the porch sleds, skis, and tricycles. Heaven.

For one moment I thought I shouldn't leave the baby alone in the car. But then I did leave her and went into the public market to buy a gallon of milk and cigarettes. I could see the car from the line beside the cash register and craned my neck up to catch sight of the door. Then I bought the stuff, paid the woman and stepped out into the glaring sunlight. I went to the car, looked in the window and saw the car seat and the baby were gone.

I looked into the car everywhere, at first sure I was making some mistake. Memory, or expectation. Something must be wrong with me. Maybe I left the baby at home. But the blood in my body grew cold. I looked up and down the street, where two mothers with carriages were walking. I went to them and said did you see someone take a baby out of that car. No dear, she said and turned away. And I asked a passing man who appeared and he said Sorry, honey. And I knew then that it was Honey who had come and taken my child.

I drove right off to the police who said they would do their best, but no one could find her, she was gone from my arms, hands and sleep, a vanished presence, my blood. And it was all over the news, a search for witnesses and two people said they had, in fact, seen a pretty young woman in a gold lamé dress and honey-blonde hair, carrying a baby in a basket, and how odd they thought it was, at the time, that a woman would carry a baby like that, like fruit and vegetables, down the street; and they found the car seat in a garbage pail behind the supermarket and inspected the garbage for the corpse of the baby, but found none. Phones kept ringing with people saying how they had seen this woman with a baby in a basket, one in Tampa and one in El Paso, one in Nebraska and one in Maine, one in Truth and Consequences and one in Tulane. And since there was no ransom demand, some people accused me of simple carelessness and others accused me of hiding the baby myself; but the majority kindly begged me to appear on television, crying, so they could get the dope of my emotions.

So I complied and described the strawberry mark on her spine, her brown eyes, her big nose and small ears. She was a baby who rarely cried, I said, but when she wriggles around it means she wants to be changed, and she eats four meals a day: oatmeal and applesauce at eight, mashed peas and minced beef at twelve, peaches and rice at five and a bowl of ice cream before bed at eight. And she usually wakes around midnight when you can give her a bottle please, but be sure to hold her while you do it, don't just toss the bottle in the crib with her; and rock her if she is unhappy, she is very docile and only wants what she needs, but sometimes she just likes to be rocked or sung to. Yes, she loves music, and she sleeps when she's in the car with the radio on (and be sure not to leave her alone in the car if you need to go shopping, don't let the sun get in her eyes). She was born eight months ago, and I only stopped nursing her recently, so she should be immune to some things, but she'll need her next vaccination in a couple of weeks.

The cameras moved off; the world news came on. They

left me standing at my door, trailed off dragging their equipment behind them. Some people were appalled by the rational nature of my speech, others were perplexed. A few sent me money and sympathy. It was on a Sunday afternoon that the baby was discovered by two twelve-year-old boys. They were going fishing in the woods near my house. They heard a crow, they thought it was a baby crying and trod across the soft pine needles under the somnolent arch of redwood. Dark and dappling light. A sweet smell. The crow flew up just where the baby lay in a straw basket. A fairy tale. She was lying very still. It's a doll, said Arthur. No, it's real, said Jim. They walked in terror closer and saw flies buzzing around her. (She had not been changed for ages.) She was quiet. Her eyes were open to the trees overhead. Her hands were folded across her belly. Is it dead? asked Arthur. I don't know, said Jim, I want to go home. We better tell, said Arthur, Mom. So they ran through the woods to Arthur's house and his mother came running back with them, her apron strings flying, a bosomy woman with gray hair. The boys followed trembling. (Jim's mother was down at the Plaza shopping.) This was no squeamish mother, Lord be praised, she went right up to the basket, hissing the flies away, unoffended by the heavy stench of shit that hung over the baby. She leaned down and picked the whole basket up and looked into the baby's narrow face. It's not dead, but it's not normal either, she said. She carried the basket down the path in the direction of my house, which was a quarter of a mile down. She carried the basket into the kitchen, calling my name and I ran in from the empty nursery, but didn't want to look at the baby. So the mother changed and washed her, while the boys called the hospital and the cops. The mother dipped the baby in the kitchen sink, warm water, and soaped her, but the baby didn't make a sound or a motion, and when she was dressed in fresh green pajamas and looked halfway like the baby I knew, I tore open my blouse and shoved my breast against her lips. But the lips were pale and still, the eyes glassy. The mother was looking for a bottle when the ambulance came and a young man pried the baby away from me. But the mother said give it back, so he did, and I went along for the ride to the hospital. I wanted Arthur's mother to come with me, but Arthur wanted her to stay with him, he was crying; so she did stay with him, which was only natural. All was well, all will be well.

In real life Gusty has wild thick hair, with a silvery undertone. His face is narrow, his nose straight, his lips delicate, and when he smiles, he is all creases. It is the smoothness of his brow, not a line, which gives his eyes their remarkable glare. A slender throat, prominent collarbone, a narrow smooth chest and ingrown belly-button. His arms are slender with narrow veins, his legs are nobby. He walks with his hand under my elbow, as if I were in need of support, moving slowly, lazily. We are seen everywhere together. My hair is thick, short and black, my body tiny but bosomy. I come to his shoulder.

He wears baggy clothes that give him the air of a shell-shocked soldier returned from the Second World War. People glance at him cautiously, he could be crazy. Who would guess that I am the one trembling with anxieties, claustrophobia, agoraphobia, fear of people, falling objects, heights, tunnels, bridges, closed doors, breathing? No one who used to see me carrying radical literature into bookstores. He drove me out of coffee shops, now, with his references to schizophrenia and mental disease. The very words filled my bowels with terror. I would run home, leaving him with a book by Wilhelm Reich or some other brain twister. And the more hysterical I became, the better he liked it, cross-examining me about my state of mind, my history, Alice and Henry, and, of course, Honey.

Was she pretty then? he might ask or: Was she obsessed with sex? I floundered between a perverse desire to reunite the two (thereby freeing myself from both) and the equally perverse desire to hang onto him. All my wishes were perverse in his terms. And my money was running out at the same rate as my sanity.

One day, when Gusty had gone to his classes, I snuck into his room and began to pry among his possessions for the sign that would break my attachment to him. The emotions involved in this activity were not as simple as they would have been before I had done my political work. Then they would have been motivated only by jealousy and the yen for his love; now they carried political traces. I viewed him as my enemy in every sense. I mistrusted his deeds far more than his feelings for me; mistrusted the entire ethical structure on which he hung his sanity. Stealing around his room filled me, therefore, with a confusion of emotions – part personal, part political. I didn't want him to leave me, I wanted to leave him. But if he was going to do it first, I wanted the evidence of his rottenness way in advance, I wanted to know how and why to hate him. In a near rapturous state of anxiety I plunged my hands into his deskful of papers. It was only a moment before I had the evidence.

A letter to Honey describing me by name, and by my involvement in radical activities. He belittled me and them. He was even racist. I scrawled down your address in New York and ran upstairs, triumphant, energized by the evidence.

So what's your problem now? he kept asking.

Nothing, nothing.

You really should see a shrink, I swear.

So should you, I sneered.

What for?

You always seem miserable. You hate the world.

Wouldn't you if you were me and you were you and we were we?

Hey, I said that to you yesterday.

One day a letter came to him from you. I saw it first: your unmistakable round and childish script, red ink. I held it up to him under a windy sky. Gray clouds scudded overhead.

I guess I'll go home for Christmas, was his only comment.

He didn't make love to me now that you were back in touch with him. He sat around my room, reduced to behaving like an ordinary person. His guilt made him polite, kind, and even his vocabulary changed, so that now he used words like love and happiness instead of libido and projection.

I guess I'll go home for Christmas too, I remarked.

Home?

And so deliberately with the same amount of money – two-hundred-and-ten dollars – in my pocket, I left for the east coast by bus. I was nameless for that journey and carried one suitcase and a bag of books.

Imagine, if you can, the extraordinary state of mind I was in. Five years had passed between my leaving the east and coming west. I had managed to isolate myself, like a biological culture, from the society I knew best. I was more than an exile. I really didn't exist. All my talents, small as they were, had to be laid to rest in order to simply survive. No one wanted me or needed me now. I might have been an old woman or a tree in a desert. It came down to that. I considered disposing of myself, for my body was a hindrance and no joy nested in my limbs. I had stopped perceiving the future as a distant point in space toward which I advanced, day by day; and instead I saw the days advancing towards me like a thug at war, huge bodies of space to defend myself (impossibly) against.

There was no decision to be made. I had to move, just as you have to wake up when sleep is completed. So I did and returned to the place I had first come from bearing my two large bags, having said goodbye to no one. It did occur to me to call Sal for a ride but that seemed complicated, and more terrifying than my isolation. One name lay in my mouth, on my palate, a name which had lain there, unspoken, but tasted, all along. If he should come to look for me, finally, and find me completely gone, there would be no hope of our ever meeting again. So, in a telephone booth at the bus terminal, laden down with coins, I tried to uncover a trail leading to Heaven and called an acquaintance of his in San Francisco. This fellow told me to call someone called Joyce who told me to call Larry who wasn't there but whose friend Jay said to call Roger who said he had a phone number I could try in Santa Fe. And I rang that number and a woman said Heaven was expected back in town in a week or so.

What is he doing now? I asked.

What was he doing then? she asked. Music and stuff.

Oh no, he's got some money now. Are you his wife? She laughed in a roar, no, and asked for my name and we said goodbye. (Just today I happened to see a picture in a book of Botticelli prints of a man named Giuliano de Medici – brother of Lorenzo the Magnificent – who looks just like my Heaven.)

I felt almost euphoric having located his position on the map and boarded the bus for the long haul east. On this journey I met no one. The bus was, fortunately, empty enough for me to maintain my isolation almost all the way across. Snow, snow. It had been five years since I had seen it and I pressed my cheek against the glass, giving myself to the pain it gave me, willingly. Most people may not understand, but there are times when feelings of excess heat and cold, or wetness or wind, are to be pursued. Not the perfect temperature, the most comfortable seat; not the easiest route, or the quietest corner; but just the opposite. The less comfortable I was, the closer to pleasure I came. I would have been happiest out in that whirling blizzard, without stockings or gloves, fastened by the harsh sensations to an unassailable space locked away inside myself. But there I was, inside the bus, for better or worse, bouncing east.

Now you are probably wondering why I was moving in that direction, given all the others I could have taken. I didn't know then and I don't want to pretend I know why now. I was grateful for the snow and the slow journey. I did not want to go insane. It would call attention to me, and that was the last thing I desired. No human attention or confinement for me. I had no faith in psychiatry or doctors of any kind, which would force me to face them. On the contrary, I feared them as enemies of my freedom. Camus was my lover and hero and guide for that time. He was so alive in his notebooks! But I also had put a crack in my consciousness and air from eternity was pouring in.

I arrived at the old Gloucester Street house around five in the evening. A thin coat of slush under my wet shoes. I was ice cold. My bags were at the bus terminal and I held my thin coat close around me, chilled to the bone. There were yellow lights in the windows. Streetlights, car lights, and rush-hour traffic, held up by poor weather. I didn't hesitate but went up the steps and rang the doorbell. I could see a potted palm in the corner of the living room, books and dun-colored furniture. The door opened on a girl of about fourteen, wearing a blue sweater and shirt, her blonde hair shoulder-length.

I'm looking for the Casements, I told her.

The Casements?

They used to live here, I think, I said.

Hey Mummy! she yelled. Didn't those people who lived here before us die?

The mother, strict, tall, Germanic, appeared in the dim frame of our kitchen door.

Who is it?

Someone looking for the Casements.

The mother came forward in pale green. She looked me over but didn't ask me in.

They haven't lived here for years, she told me. I believe they were killed, tragically, in an air crash. Are you an old friend of theirs? They had no living children.

I just wanted to know if it was true, I said and went down the steps.

It wasn't a long walk to the bus terminal, but I was bitterly cold and unable to pause to enjoy my misery. I had seventy-two dollars left in my purse. I could only go so far. I stood on the corner of Commonwealth Avenue watching the lights beam down and pass. Then I trudged on to the bus terminal and checked my bag out of its locker, getting the schedule for the morning before I went outside again. There was a crowd waiting for cabs. I stood with them, letting others go before me, one after the other, as my mind searched out a destination. I decided, finally, on the hotel where Honey's father used to keep his mysterious mistress, and I grabbed the next cab. Christmas, I noticed, was all over.

It was strange to find myself absolutely alone in such a luxurious room. Warm and golden. Incapable of much pleasure, still, I began to feel a recurrence of tension, tics in my calves, rushes of panic and I took from my bag a little bottle of Kahlúa given me by Gusty. A hot bath, where I watched my skin for twitches, as if for insects, and long tiny slugs from the nip bottle. If I looked out

the hotel window, the familiar streets and brick build-
ings gazed back at me mournfully. If I confined my view
to the room itself, I felt the stuffiness overwhelming me.
I sat on my bed, insane, staring at the telephone. So
many people out there who knew me. Had they
searched? Had they listed me officially as missing? What
would any of them do if they recognized me now?

In those days morning, which had before been my happiest time, was the grimmest part of the day. I awoke to
fear, ghosts of my arms raised to ward off other ghosts.
Inside myself there lived such gross emotions, I could
only imagine a coffin as the bed I deserved. The only
way to survive myself was by motion, for if I lay still too
long in bed, I would become paralyzed or be overcome
by anguish. So I rushed around, breathing hard, and
even took some swallows from a bottle of paregoric. It
was sickening, but did the trick.

I went down to the desk and asked the man there if a
Miss Jane Tabor was still registered in the hotel. Jane
Tabor, your father's mistress, and a name I would never
forget. (Those names we learn in early youth, even the
most casual mentions, have this strange effect. The
name Jane Tabor might have been Milky Way or Sem-
piternal Rose, because I never saw her.) We had hung
about this same lobby, years before, trying to guess
which one she might be. We were even kicked out of the
place once for loitering.

Miss Tabor, certainly, said the octogenarian desk clerk. She's still here. Won't be back till five-fifteen. Gone to work.

I ventured brooding through the cold streets. I had about forty-five dollars left. In spite of my nervous condition I had acquired a kind of street sense that lent me direction. No one would know that I was anything but a nobody minding her own business and not thinking too hard about anything. The sky was streaked with the coming snow, yellowish, yeasty. I hastened to catch a subway fast. But first I bought a notebook and a Bic pen.

I was sitting on the subway underground, halfway between Harvard and Central, when the thing jammed to a stop. The conductor walked by. The people around murmured and turned to their own reflections on the black glass. A dirty car. I was struck with the familiar fever of dread and glanced at the woman beside me. She was plumpish, youngish, softish, rougey, bleach-blonde, perfumed, polished, probably a salesgirl. She wore two rings, a diamond and a gold band. I stared at her calm and dimpled fingers resting on her black patent leather bag. She smiled at me and said *Tsch*. I was pleased by this comradely comment and turned her into my wife. After all, I must do something to protect myself. What would it be like to be a man with a nice wife? Say we have two children at home. Her mother takes care of them in her lace curtain two-family near Inman Square. We both work. We sometimes meet for lunch, though I don't like to mix business with pleasure. I'm a superintendent in a new block of apartments in Kenmore Square. She sells lingerie a block away. I'm always soothed by her presence. Her soft skin, which will soon be fat, is the marshmallow lining around my prickly days. I have no future, and I know this, but she, Vera, is so good to me, it doesn't matter. She is unassailable. I bring home enough cash to keep us in a little two-bedroom place near her mother. And her mother is a dream. She takes care of our children while we work. We're putting all of Vera's income into savings which we'll put down on a house in three years. Her mother just loves those kids. She has a hot meal for all of us at the end of the day. When we go home, the kids are tired, and ready to hit the hay, so we can relax in bed with Fritos and beer and watch the tube. So what have I got to be scared of? She's beside me! She won't let anything hurt me! And her mother! She's making chili for supper. What a life! I'm happy! I will never go insane!

I sat in the Public Gardens near the statue of George Washington, who radiated turquoise, who might have been dragged from the bottom of the sea. This color, in the gray of the day, blazed. Slush, dark brick, slush. Home is where the hurt is. I looked at Boston. I was crying. Up Commonwealth Avenue, there were no leaves or magnolia or flowering cherry, but unlimited gloom. I was planning on going to your house and ringing the bell. That house might contain the information I sought, since I felt like a lady detective in pursuit of one hidden fact which would blow the case apart. A mirror facing the sky, it would shatter if I lowered my face to look in. The important thing was to avoid aggression, to sit and listen, pay attention and when the constellation of accidents looked right, move; but not before.

I moved when the first flake of snow struck my fist. And soon I stood in the hall of your decaying mansion. Your mother dropped my coat on the floor and talked about the weather. She smelled.

Mary, everyone thought you were dead, she said.

But she could say this to anyone, I knew, whom she had not seen for years. A pickled brain is short on facts. I was lucky. Your father, had he been there, would have blanched, staggered, and called the cops when he saw me. But I had cased the joint. I knew he wasn't home anymore. Gusty told me he had died.

She padded, then, down the hall to the familiar filthy

kitchen and I gasped at the stink of cat shit, refusing to eat or drink.

Could we sit in the living room? I asked.

We ended up there, thankfully, me smoking and she drinking brandy and soda. It must have been noon or after. I saw snowflakes, now, gathering behind a pot of dead ivy on the windowsill. Your mother's face was like a rag that has been used on the floor. I could hardly look at her.

Where's Honey these days? I asked.

Honey Honey Honey, she mused, racking her brain.

Is she still in the hospital? I suggested.

Oh no, no, no, she said. Oh no, no.

Around here?

Oh no. She's doing music now, the recorder, in a little group, in New York. Music. Music. Poor Honey. You girls. I'll never forget ... poor Honey.

Why? She sounds fine.

Oh no, never, not Honey, never.

Why not?

She touched her temple with her glass trembling.

It's hereditary, you know, she said. My father was as mad as a hatter, and my brother too. She should never marry. And of course there was the question of her own father ...

Suddenly I wanted to throw up, it would be no problem, I left her for the bathroom and did it. Helped along by the cat box which was there, reeking behind the kitchen in that greasy cubicle.

In the mirror my face was the color of the mirror, ashy.

I better go, I told her, home.

Where's home now? I'll tell Honey.

I'm not sure, I said.

Call her. She's in the book, she said. New York phone book.

She looked at the snow in the doorway behind me.

Jesus Christ, I hate these New England winters. Fifty-eight of them – that's enough.

We said goodbye casually; it was as if none of it ever happened, not the day or the life.

Oh fire oh wind oh salt off the sea oh rain oh trees oh sand oh bush, oh winter oh brick oh steam oh steel oh lights aluminum plastic and snow. From Chelsea to Charlestown to Everett, Allston, Southie, the Hill and North End, the subways grinding underground. Trolleys on rails, statues on stones, smells of cod fishcakes steaming up from basements, shipyards, the Constitution, the Mystic River Bridge in a swath of white snow. Where would I go and deposit my body now? My only hope was hidden in a little white graveyard next to Christ Church reserved for the long ago dead, or the Cambridge Common near the hotel. Help will come, I shout into myself. Oh no, not this time, is the reply, you've been too sure of yourself this time. I sat on the neat little bed and ordered a drink. I drank it in front of the window, my stomach rolling, my mind traveling where my body couldn't go, not yet. Heaven help me.

Where are you? I hear him say in my head.

In a hotel.

Take a train and I'll meet you.

Why not fly?

You don't have enough money. What then?

Don't keep worrying about the future! Take a hot bath, have a drink, read a book of poems – Rilke or an anthology will do under the circumstances, then get some music into you, a radio, thcn when you're all clean, and living in the present, write your life story down, then hop in a cab to the station and start moving. I'll be there. I'll wire you some cash. Now do what I say.

I turned on the bath and steamed in it for a long time, ordered another drink, but I had no poems or radio. It was going to be time soon, anyway, to see the woman, and I was pleasantly high now and quite content to run a conversation with myself.

Do telephones work? How? I asked myself.

I have no idea how they work.

Was that really Heaven or just his voice?

It was his voice, I replied to myself.

How did it get through the air to me?

You're hearing things.

I need to talk to someone.

Jane Tabor.

What'll I do then? I said.

Well, that depends on what she's like. You mustn't hope she's going to help you. Give you money or a job or anything. She might not even want to talk to you. You know what happens every time you hope for something. Or pray. So knock wood a hundred times. Okay. Now think of all the good things we'll do tomorrow.

Like what?

The train. New York.

I don't have enough money.

The bus.

I don't think so.

We may have to leave this hotel without paying.

I know. I've thought of that.

What name did you give at the desk?

I can't remember!

It was some movie star.

No, no, it was Eve Saint.

Well, that's almost a movie star.

I'm scared.

Remember you are a revolutionary not a movie star.

Fearfully I knocked on the door on the fourth floor of the Hotel Continental.

Who is it? she called.

Just – uh – someone, no one you know.

She opened the door, anyway, and looked me over. Yes?

My name is – uh – Debbie Reynolds, I told her,

ha-ha, believe it or not. Anyway, I'm a friend of Honey Figgis. And I wonder if you know where she is and what happened to her.

She looked faintly surprised and suspicious, but forgivingly she let me in.

Honey Figgis, she said. Why would I know?

I just thought you might.

Gracious, was her comment.

This is a beautiful suite, I said.

Sweet it was, golden, luxurious, clean and soft, a starlight Hollywood fantasy. She settled me on a small white sofa. Would you like a drink, dear? I always have a sip of sherry after work.

Yes, please.

She was not the striped trout I imagined, named Jane Tabor, she was small and Spanish in appearance. Thick black hair tied back on her neck, bright red lips, and almond-shaped eyes. She was dressed in an orange Italian-knit suit. A woman who could take care of herself, who would hold things together and be called a bitch for it.

Honey Figgis, she said, sitting beside me.

She was my best friend in school.

Well, this is the strangest thing.

Why?

I was just thinking about her last night.

Mentally I corrected her and bet she was thinking of the father, pompous, cruel and sexual, looming in the shadows of that suite.

And what were you thinking?

Don't whisper, speak up.

Her father.

Well, yes, but no it was Honey, she insisted. I was listening to Flamenco.

So?

For some reason it reminded me of Ramon, her first husband.

I can see why.

She smiled cheerfully, refolding her legs and dipping into her glass of sherry.

He was awfully attractive, wasn't he?

But Honey had a breakdown. After the divorce. A very serious breakdown.

But she's okay now?

Apparently she is playing with some wind quartet, so I guess so.

Did you ever know her friend Mary, in high school? I asked.

No. She had two friends not named Mary. Libby, Henny.

Mary was a very gifted pianist, I told her. Now she's nothing.

That's sad. Your generation is sad. No guiding principles. But wait. I remember there was a girl who disappeared after her parents died. It was a huge thing here, an obvious suicide, and Honey knew her. Is that the Mary you mean?

That's the one. Did Honey care about the suicide?

Yes, of course. I believe she left her husband and came back before or after having a breakdown and trying to kill herself too. I don't know the exact timing. The madness of your generation, as Allen Ginsberg would say. Really.

Well, if she is a musician now, she must be happy. She won't be trying suicide any more.

Merry laughter from me until Jane began to ask me questions about myself.

And you, Debbie, what do you do?

I'm a Beatnik and a writer, I told her.

But really I wanted to return to my room fast. I didn't want to chat. She told me about a little dress boutique she ran in Harvard Square and I thought of asking for a job. But it was no good; the ghost of the city and my past in it was voluminous and giant. I jumped to my feet.

Why don't you speak to Jane herself? she said to me, standing.

Jane?

Jane Tabor.

I squinted through the alcohol in my veins and squeezed my little glass until it nearly burst.

Which room is she in? I asked.

Right down the hall. Two doors on the left. She's my dearest friend and she might know much more than I do, even though she stopped seeing the father years before he died. Honey and his past, you know, it was too much. Too much for everyone. For her, for Honey, for his family, I'm sure, too, don't get me wrong. I'm sure you understand.

That night and the next day I sat in my golden hotel room and wrote down everything you are reading here, from page one to now.

It was dark when I put my bag outside the door. The desk clerk followed me.

I'm looking for a cab, I told him.

Checking out now?

I'll just get a cab and come right back.

The phone rang at the desk and he hobbled back to get it. Was I shaking? Yes. Waiting, cold in my feet, for a cab, which was a long time coming, to let out a silvery woman (probably the real Jane!) and I threw in my bag and leaped in when she was out.

To the Greyhound Terminal, I told the driver.

And we were off and crawling through the traffic. Lights, clacking chains, the slap of the windshield wiper was my heartbeat. I had gotten away with not paying! Ethics and time seem to be in bondage to each other.

In New York I had to shoplift my food and sleep on a bench in the Port Authority. My feet were soaking, I was filthy and tired, and finally I used the address for Honey I found in the phonebook and walked there. The sorrow boiling inside me kept me warm, I think, because I remember standing under the awning of her building, with my coat wide open and a wind lashing at my throat, and feeling flying drops as if they were sweat.

If Heaven hadn't told me that people who have murdered always look as if they have died, I might have killed her with his toy pearl-handled gun. But the inescapable empathy buried in that fact disarmed me and anyway it was not my style to kill.

Honey was wearing a lumpish cap, her hair fell out of it in strands, her eyes were enormously ringed with mascara, she was shuffling through the rain with her coat flapping open. She had gained about thirty pounds and had the slothful movements of someone heavily medicated. Grey stone eyes, as if she had traveled too many trips on weighted rafts crossing the North Sea from Holland to Hull, making her hair straight, the offspring of murderous but lost Vikings. So her history too was brought home to me: down the chute of my gaze she came like a dry case of reality. I felt the bang at the bottom as if afloat in bar-colored cognac. It's a man's world.

She – sister, friend, mother! – didn't even recognize me in the flash of time I allowed for it. She slouched past, her dull eyes grazed my face and shoulder, then out beyond, she pressed her fingers to a yawn and paused to pull her keys from her bag. I gawked from an angle halfway behind where she didn't see me because my body was in her past while she stayed poised in my present. Her lips moved around in concentration as they do with people who have dry mouths from excess medication.

Someone dragged a Christmas tree past and inside the building, so I surmised Christmas hadn't come yet. Had Halloween? Had Thanksgiving? No, it was November 21, 1963, I found out the next day.

Heaven, I tell you, I began in those twenty-four hours to become all of a piece. The location of history may be in my cells, but the individual soul lives across space, skinless and free. Gaudy wings of the angelic orders must transport us in some way.

First you have to try on the colors and then you have to let them go and be a blend, a conjunction.

You speed across time and years and still remain a fixed entity. Far below are the bodies of your identities, they are not the same. But like a minuscule stack of clothing.

All along I had the question backwards. *Did anyone love me?* It should have been, Did I love anyone? Yes, I loved five. I loved Henry and Alice and Heaven and Honey and Sal. Not one of us was related by blood to the other. Why did I judge them so harshly? Why couldn't I have cried out to them: *Love me, oh Love whom I love!*

That's what you cry when you find there's no fracture in the grammar of heart and mind. That's what the dying cry. I think every person is a perfect creation. Selfish and in agony that person still persists in its integrity.

That day I turned my face and then my body and walked in circles around one block after another and finally ended back in front of the same door and the doorman. I handed him this bundle of writing and told him to please give it to you.

If I could ever see you again, I would begin our friendship and this whole story with these words: A point of view is the only reward for suffering. That's why it's so hard to give up.

Also available from grand**IOTA**

APROPOS JIMMY INKLING
Brian Marley

In a Westminster café-cum-courtroom, Jimmy Inkling is on trial, perhaps for his life. Unless, of course, he's dead already. But will that be enough to prevent him from eliminating those who give evidence against him?

978-1-874400-73-8   318pp

WILD METRICS
Ken Edwards

1970s London: short-life communal living, the beginnings of the alt-poetry scene, not forgetting sex, drugs and rock'n'roll. Forty years on: where have the wild metrics of those days taken us? This prose extravaganza dives into the inscrutable forking paths of memory, questions what poetry is, and concludes that the author cannot know what he is doing.

978-1-874400-74-5   244pp

THE GREY AREA
Ken Edwards

A mystery novel in which the mystery seems incapable of any single solution. The action takes place in a mythical, contemporary English setting near the coast, and on the edge of a vast marsh. The detective charged with solving the mystery is an illegal resident in a business park. His assistant is more concerned with her seven-year-old son who is failing at school. It's poetry by other means.

978-1-874400-76-9   328pp

Production of this book has been made possible with the help of the following individuals and organisations who subscribed in advance:

Peter Bamfield
Chris Beckett
Charles Bernstein
Lillian Blakey
Andrew Brewerton
Ian Brinton
Jasper Brinton
Peter Brown
Norma Cole
Claire Crowther
Beverly Dahlen
Rachel DuPlessis
Ian Durant
Elaine Edwards
Allen Fisher/Spanner
Jim Goar
Paul A Green
Paul Griffiths
Charles Hadfield
John Hall
Andrew Hamilton
Randolph Healy
Rob Holloway
Anthony Howell
Peter Hughes
Romana Huk
Pierre Joris
Richard Makin
Colleen McCallion

Aodhan McCardle
Michael Mann
Shelby Matthews
Askold Melnyczuk
Mark Mendoza
Peter Middleton
Joe Milazzo
David Miller
John Muckle
John Olson
Irene Payne
Sean Pemberton
Simon Perril
Lou Rowan
Sad Press
Michael Schmidt
Maurice Scully
Hazel Smith
Valerie Soar
Harriet Tarlo
Pam Thompson
Keith Tuma
Keith Washington
Susan Wheeler
June Wilkes
John Wilkinson
Tyrone Williams

4 x anon

www.grandiota.co.uk